LAMPER'S MEADOW

LAMPER'S MEADOW

Barbra Minar

CROSSWAY BOOKS • WHEATON, ILLINOIS
A DIVISION OF GOOD NEWS PUBLISHERS

For Steven, Jeffrey,
and Katherine Minar
and in memory of
Christin Evangel Meeks

Lamper's Meadow.

Copyright © 1992 by Barbra Minar.

Published by Crossway Books, a division of
Good News Publishers, 1300 Crescent St., Wheaton, Illinois 60187.

Cover illustration: Jeff Haynie

First printing, 1992

Printed in the United States of America

Library of Congress Cataloging-in-Publication Data
Minar, Barbra.
    Lamper's meadow / Barbra Minar.
        p.   cm.
        Summary: Two children are transported through the light of a
prism into Lamper's Meadow, a kingdom inhabited by very special
animals, where they must help fight the powers of darkness.
        [1. Fantasy.   2. Christian life—Fiction.]   I. Title.
PZ7.M65165Lam 1992   [Fic]—dc20   91-34151
ISBN 0-89107-663-8

00	99	98	97	96	95	94	93	92
15	14	13	12	11	10	9	8	7	6	5	4	3	2	1

*"And God saw
that the light was good,
and God separated the light
from the darkness."*

GENESIS 1:4

CONTENTS

THE EXPERIMENT

ANDREW JERKED HIS blue corduroy cap down hard over his blond hair. Narrowing his eyes behind his thick glasses, he stared out his upstairs bedroom window at his cousin Sara. She sat leaning against his California oak tree reading a thick book.

How could Mom do this to me, he thought. *Asking Miss Know-It-All here for the whole summer! It's only been two days, and she's driving me bats with all her questions. It feels like she's been here two YEARS! Well, she's NOT going to get in the way of my work.*

Andrew's fingers lightly swung his small cut-glass prism dangling in the window. The prism caught the hot sunlight, bent it, and sent dancing yellow, blue, and red rainbows splashing across the room. For a few moments he watched, almost hypnotized by the shifting colors and light. In his mind he lifted weightlessly off the floor and into the air. Reaching out, he grabbed a light beam with both hands, swung himself up on it, and shot like a missile right through his wall. Cold wind stung his face as he streaked over the California coastline, through summer sky, past the stars, and into deep, black space. His daydreams broke. He looked down at Sara. *Rats! I wish she'd missile away somewhere. Anywhere!*

Lifting the twirling prism by the string, he slipped it over his head and tucked it under his red T-shirt. Andrew pulled on his high-top tennis shoes and bounded down the stairs two at a time.

He yanked open the front door and slammed it. Sara jumped. Dropping her book in the grass, she stood up, feet wide apart, and put her small hands on her hips like a drill sergeant. "Do you have to be so loud? You scared me to death!" Her green eyes flashed under a mop of short, dark hair.

"Sorry," said Andrew. "I'm just in a hurry."

"Well," said Sara pointing her finger at his high-tops, "you better tie your laces, or you're going to fall on your face."

"Better get used to it. This isn't Ohio. *Nobody* ties their shoe laces here in California. I got to split. See you later," said Andrew.

"Where are you going?" asked Sara.

"Got things to do," he replied, walking down the street with long-legged strides.

"Hey, wait a minute," said Sara, hurrying behind him. "I'm pretty bored around here. I'll go with you."

The back of Andrew's neck burned. *How come I'm stuck with a girl following me down the street! I wish I'd grabbed my skateboard,* he thought. *Then I could really move out.*

Sara began running. A surprising foghorn voice blasted

out of her small body. "WAIT UP, ANDREW. You know your mom said for you to show me around."

Andrew slowed down. "O.K., but shut up, will you! You don't have to tell the whole world!" Galloping behind Andrew, Sara asked questions like popcorn. Andrew walked as fast as he could.

"Where are we going?" asked Sara

"If you've got to know, I'm going down to Mr. Maxwell's basement," said Andrew.

"Who's he?"

"Mr. Maxwell was a science teacher at Belfield High, but he got old and quit," said Andrew.

"I'm sure you mean he retired. What are you doing in his basement?" asked Sara.

"Some scientific stuff—about color and light," said Andrew.

"I know all about light," said Sara. "Light travels 186,280 miles a second. I read about it in volume 7 of my *World Book of Science.* Light is one of many different kinds of electromagnetic radiations—disturbances that travel through the universe in the form of waves."

"O.K., brain machine, what do you know about prisms?" asked Andrew.

"I know that when white sunlight passes through a prism, the prism bends the light waves at different angles. That produces color," said Sara.

"I guess you know *everything*," said Andrew.

"I can't help it if I'm smart. You're just jealous. Is it much farther?" Sara was panting.

"If you can't keep up, you better go back," said Andrew running a little faster.

"No way!" Sara's loud voice blasted Andrew from the back. "I can keep up!"

"O.K, O.K. Just promise you won't bug me. I'm going to work on an important experiment," said Andrew, shoving his glasses up the bridge of his narrow nose.

"Well, it's probably good I'm with you. You might get yourself in trouble."

Oh great, thought Andrew.

Suddenly Andrew stopped beside an overgrown box-wood hedge. He pointed to a kid-size hole in the dense thicket.

"This way." Andrew slipped his lanky body through the space with Sara right at his heels. Once on the other side, they stood up in the backyard of a large yellow house. The white shutters hung slightly crooked, making the windows look tired. "Sure needs paint. Looks sort of spooky," said Sara standing behind him.

"Don't be a jerk. Mr. Maxwell just has better things to do than paint his house." Andrew rapped hard on the back door. "Mr. Maxwell. Mr. Maxwell!"

"He's not home," said Sara shifting her weight from one small foot to the other. "Now what?"

"Just go into the basement. I have permission," he said, jumping off the step and running around the side of the house. "Here's the door. Come on if you're coming."

Andrew walked down three cement steps and pushed the heavy wooden door open. Pulling a long string, he clicked on a single light bulb, making it swing back and forth, casting long shadows in the corners.

Sara put her nose in the air and sniffed. "Smells sort of . . ."

"Musty," said Andrew.

"And it STINKS," said Sara.

"It's the chemicals. We do chemistry experiments in here," said Andrew.

"I took a special chemistry class for gifted students last year," said Sara. Andrew groaned.

"Wow! Look at all the stuff in here!" Sara's eyes explored the room.

Large cardboard boxes stood stacked to the ceiling. A broken table lamp leaned against a wall beside a large antique picture frame. Saws, hammers, screwdrivers, paint cans, and bottles and jars filled with nails lined wooden shelves. A roll of baling wire hung on a rusty spike. Dusty trays of test tubes, wire baskets, and three bird cages sat on tables and wooden crates. From the ceiling hung everything from baskets to bicycles. A large red and white wall clock, buzzing as the black hands traveled around the face, was plugged into an outlet on the back wall. It was 3:50 P.M.

Andrew moved his lean body through boxes and old furniture to the only clear section in the basement.

"This is what I like," he said, pulling out a long wooden drawer from beneath a table. "Mr. Maxwell stores his special science equipment in here. We've got test tubes, burners, and—"

"But where's your big experiment?" asked Sara. Andrew glared at her.

"I can't think if you're going to bug me. Promise me, no more questions," said Andrew.

"All right. But I can't help it if I've got lots of questions!" Sara poked out her full bottom lip and slumped against the work table.

She watched Andrew lift a long, black felt bag from the drawer. Pulling open the drawstring, he took out two tall prisms. He stood one prism on the table in front of him. From a brown case underneath the table, he lifted out an old projector with a long extension cord. Plugging in the projector, he snapped it on. Then he switched off the single basement light.

"What are you doing?" asked Sara.

"Shhh!" said Andrew. "No questions. You promised!"

He began adjusting the light from the projector. Finding its target, the light hit the prism. Vibrant yellow, red, green, violet, and blue exploded through on the other side.

"That's BEAUTIFUL!" said Sara. "What about the other prism?"

"First—you see that pure light going through the prism breaks up into all the colors," Andrew said in a scientific voice.

"Second—I must place the two prisms the right distance apart." He set up the second prism on another table across the room.

"Third—I will re-collect the colors through the second prism and make pure light again."

"WOW! Just like it says in my *World Book of Science*," Sara said. Walking in between the two prisms, Sara let the yellow, red, green, violet, and blue colors cover her body. "Look! My jeans are yellow!"

"I need one more thing to collect the colors. I put a big screen with a tiny hole in the middle between the prisms. Do you see it?" asked Andrew feeling around for the screen. "Mr. Maxwell usually keeps the screen right here. Rats! I can't find it."

"So much for your scientific experiment," said Sara. "You must have a light going through two prisms set the right distance apart and a screen with the perfect-size hole in between them."

"Okay, brains. Just hang on. Maybe I can make something else work. Hand me that old picture frame," Andrew requested. "I bet I can make a screen out of that."

"You'd have to cut a hole exactly right," said Sara.

"I *know* that," replied Andrew.

"Ick! I hate spiders," Sara said, poking cobwebs from the picture frame with the toe of her shoe. She picked up the wooden frame and sneezed as thick dust flew everywhere. Holding the frame up in the rainbow of colors, she tried to get a better look. The glass in the frame reflected back the bands of red, blue, and green.

Sara brushed some dirt off the glass. Something underneath the glass caught her attention. "Hey, I think I see a picture." She rubbed harder. "I can't quite make it out."

Andrew moved closer. He shoved up his glasses, squinting hard at the picture. Through the glass, Andrew began to make out black eyes and a flat wide snout on a silvery surface. "It looks like some sort of animal. Yeah, I think I see whiskers."

"HEY!" Sara boomed, "THIS IS HOT!" Dropping the frame, Sara shook her fingers hard and jammed them in her mouth.

"Sara, *look!*" whispered Andrew. "*Look!*" He pointed wildly. "Look at the frame—" It floated in the air in front of them. Sara gasped and grabbed onto Andrew's arm. Suddenly, a high-pitched crunch sounded through the room as the glass cracked. Sharp splinters crashed to the basement floor. Trembling, Sara and Andrew clung together in the center of the color beam. They stood between the two prisms—eyes glued to the sight.

"There IS an animal in there," said Sara. "A big rodent." Then the animal's fur began glowing with a radiant light. The picture's silvery surface vibrated slightly. The animal's mouth opened. Sara sucked in her breath. "I think it's—trying to speak."

Four letters, like silent bubbles, blew out of the animal's mouth.

E M C O

"What's it trying to say?" whispered Andrew. "Maybe it's another language!"

"Or a word that's scrambled up," said Sara watching the letters bobbing around the strange creature's body. The *O* began to glow, making a red-hot ring. The animal faded away. The *O* grew larger and larger, filling the frame. "It's burning a hole," said Sara. "Right through the frame!"

Then the color beam pushed the children, and the intense heat from the glowing hole pulled them. Suddenly, Andrew and Sara were lifted up and sucked, along with the colors, through the hole—and straight through the second prism.

THE MEADOW AND DINK

THE LIGHT ON the other side was blinding. Sara blinked hard. Then reaching out for Andrew, she found his foot and grabbed hold.

"Andrew, look what you've done now!" Sara howled. "You and your STUPID experiments! It's like something blew us through the basement wall."

"Oh, rats! Rats!" Andrew rubbed his eyes with his fists, fighting the bright light. "My glasses are gone. I lost my glasses!" He began frantically patting the ground around him. "*Help* me, Sara! Don't just sit there. If I'm going to figure out what happened, I've got to be able to see."

"I don't know where we are, but you have to get us out of here," said Sara. She stood up, wiped her eyes with the back of her hand and gazed around. Light hit enormous dew drops. The grass, as tall and thick as a forest, sparkled as though it were crowned with diamonds.

"Wherever we are," said Andrew, "we were brought here by the light."

"What about that scary animal?" boomed Sara. "Do you think that animal is here? I think we'd better get moving. I'm ready to go home! Hey, listen." Sara cocked her head to one side. "It's music! Do you hear music?"

"I can't hear anything until I can see." Andrew pushed through the thick growth on his hands and knees feeling for his glasses.

"This is really a weird place." Sara began exploring the strange, large plants. She sniffed a stalk of king-size purple flowers. "It smells like lavender. And this silvery stuff looks like milkweed," she said, rubbing her hand over the trunk of a yellow flowering plant. "And this must be mustard, but it's as big as a tree." Just as she looked up, a giant dew drop slid down a leaf, smacking her on the face.

"OH, BROTHER! I'm completely drenched." Sara wiped her face with her shirt tail. "Look at my new shirt— and my jeans. My clothes are in shreds!" She shoved her way through the grass towards Andrew. "Wow, look at you. You're a mess! Boy, is your mom going to be mad!"

Andrew rocked back on his knees and inspected the rips in the front of his T-shirt. "Hey, what's the deal with my shirt? This shirt used to be red, and now it's white." Andrew felt for his prism around his neck. It hung safely from its string.

"Lucky I didn't lose this," he said pulling the cap off his head. "Look, it's white too. That was some trip! Tore up our clothes and sucked out the color. Hey, what's that sound?"

"I told you to listen. Come here." Sara put her ear next to a giant blade of grass. Andrew did the same.

"Wow! Sounds like a fiddle," said Andrew.

"Don't be dumb. It's a violin. If you'd studied music like

I have, you'd know these things. Listen to the milkweed. Sounds like a piccolo." She put her ear on the petal of a soft white violet. "A French horn. Everything's playing some sort of instrument. Listen down here."

Putting their ears flat to the ground, they could hear the music of the woodwinds and strings, cymbals and drums, harpsichord and brass.

"A full symphony orchestra!" said Sara.

"The Meadow's playing a classical overture," hummed a deep voice. "Nice harmony, wouldn't you say, pets?"

The children jerked their heads up and found themselves looking up at a huge, gray furry creature. Long, white whiskers twitched up and down as the creature wriggled its black nose and mouth. It stood high on strong back legs and rested back on a long, bushy tail. It peered intently at them with glistening black eyes. Its side teeth looked as sharp as two swords, and its fat cheeks bulged with food.

"HELP! A BEAST! A MONSTROUS BEAST!" screeched Sara burying her face in her hands.

For a long moment the creature stared at Andrew, and Andrew squinted back. Andrew poked Sara, but she only shivered and sniffed. *Why can't you be smart now when we need it*, he thought. Then Andrew braced himself and spoke with his best manners. "Ah—excuse me, sir, but we seem to have gotten ourselves in quite a mess. Ah—somehow we've arrived here by mistake and—"

"Mark my words. Nothing is a mistake. Everything has a purpose."

"Ah—well, then could you tell me where we are?" asked Andrew pulling nervously on the bill of his cap.

"That's why I am here, of course. To tell you that you're at the beginning."

"The beginning of what?" The creature seemed less frightening now. In fact, its deep humming voice sounded kind. And since its cheeks were already packed with food, Andrew decided it probably didn't want to eat them.

"The very beginning of everything. This is Lamper's Meadow. Oh, how rude of me. I should introduce myself. My Meadow name is Squirrel Dink. You may call me Dink, if you wish. Pray tell, what have your names been?"

"I'm Andrew Jonathan Jeffrey Stevens," Andrew answered in his strongest voice. "And this is my cousin Sara Katherine Stevens."

Sara peeked up at Dink from between her fingers. "A squirrel? A gray squirrel? You're supposed to be only eight inches tall."

"Well, of course, that's quite true." Dink puffed out his furry chest. "But here in Lamper's Meadow we grow a bit taller because of the Banquet food. Last time Mrs. Mole measured me with her tape, I was a good, full nine and a half inches."

"Oh, my! Then just how tall are we?" asked Andrew.

"Stand next to me, chappie, and we'll measure up," said Dink.

Andrew stood alongside Dink. "What do you say, Sara?" asked Andrew.

"If he's right about his own height, I'd guess you to be

only five inches, and that makes me really short," bellowed Sara. "We must have shrunk in size through the light travel. I have been pretty calm until now, Mr. Andrew Stevens. But now I am going to freak out. Do you hear me? FREAK OUT!!"

"Oh dear, dear, dear," said Dink. "You must realize that everyone in the Meadow is just the right size for themselves. Here, pet. You need a little comfort." Dink put his furry gray tail tenderly around Sara's shaking body. His warmth soon soothed her, and she buried her face in his fur.

"You know, of course, I've been sent to help you," said Dink.

"Maybe you can help me find my glasses," suggested Andrew.

"Oh, that is quite impossible. Your glasses didn't come with you," said Dink. "Glasses are useless here. You either see or—you don't see. We do need to be going. Climb on my back. I want you safe before the Snedoms fly."

"Snedoms? What are Snedoms?" asked Sara as she climbed on his back behind Andrew. She sank down in Dink's soft fur.

"I fear you may know soon enough," answered Dink.

Traveling on Dink's back was a marvelous adventure. Nestled in his fur and clinging to the squirrel's strong body, the children breezed with him down a Meadow path, scrambled over boulders, and scurried under bushes. Suddenly Dink stopped. Both Andrew and Sara grabbed onto his fur to keep from falling.

Dink pointed to an enormous dead tree. "There's one of

the places the Snedoms roost when the smoke covers the Meadow. Away from here!" Then he launched into a run with the children holding tight.

Sara wanted to ask more about these Snedoms, but a cold tingle of fear shot up her back and skull. She shivered. Swallowing her question, she grabbed Andrew even tighter around his waist as Dink sprinted like the wind.

Finally, the ride ended. "Off you go, pets. We are here."

The children slid down and stood at the end of a narrow path lined with brown and white toadstools. The path led to a dark opening in the ground.

"Where are we?" asked Andrew squinting to see.

"This is Mrs. Mole's hole. Quite a home it is, too. Mrs. Mole's expecting you."

"How weird!" said Sara. "How does she know we're here?"

"Everything that happens affects everything else," said Dink. "Your entrance into the Meadow was a big happening. No one has ever come here that way before. In fact, your entrance through the light was so extraordinary," Dink said, frowning, "that I am afraid everyone knows you're here. Follow me, chappies."

MRS. MOLE

THE CHILDREN PASSED under the tall toadstools as they followed the squirrel down the path. They stopped at the dark hole. A ring of hard-packed, black dirt circled the entrance. Swinging from a wooden post, a small sign said, "Welcome to Mrs. Mole's."

"This way now, chappies." Waving his bushy gray tail, Dink scooted into the hole. The children peered down into the darkness. Andrew narrowed his blue eyes trying to see.

"I'm not sure about this," said Andrew. "It's real black in there."

"Come along, pets. Don't fear the dark," yelled Dink from below. "I'll light the way."

"Look at Dink," said Sara staring down the hole. "He's glowing."

"Well, let's go on. We sure can't go back," said Andrew.

Together they ventured into the tunnel. They soon discovered that the darker the tunnel became, the brighter Dink became.

"Hey, look. These walls are lined with books," said Sara.

"Shelves and shelves of books. I'm glad they're civilized here. At least someone reads."

"Of course, we're civilized," said Dink, his head held high. "I say, pet!"

"Oh, Dink, I'm sorry," said Sara. "I mean—well—everything's so different."

The tunnel took a turn. As they changed directions, they heard someone singing a sweet song.

"That's Mrs. Mole. Her chamber's just ahead," said Dink.

The tunnel widened into a large, well-lit room. The shelves of books continued around the wall, making a large circle, breaking only for a white stone fireplace. The smell of honey tea drifted from a small pot hanging over a fire. Another tunnel opened on the west and another on the east.

In the center of the room a large brown mushroom served as a table. A ring of smaller mushrooms growing around it served as chairs. A three-legged stool and a spinning wheel stood by a tiny oak chest. Mrs. Mole's large magnolia leaf bed, stuffed with puffy dandelion down, stood near the fireplace.

But the most amazing sight was Mrs. Mole herself. As she sang, her soft brown velvet fur glowed with a radiant light. And her black eyes danced above a flat, wide snout dressed up with short, white whiskers. She stood slightly taller than the children. A long yellow calico apron with four deep pockets was tied neatly around her thick waist. Her song ended.

"She's the one," said Sara pulling hard on Andrew's arm.

"Who?" asked Andrew, squinting at Mrs. Mole.

"The one in the picture! Be careful." Sara's voice shook. "That rodent looks dangerous!"

"Don't be silly," said Andrew. "You can't be right." But in his heart he feared Sara spoke the truth.

"Hello, my children, welcome to Lamper's Meadow." Mrs. Mole held out her broad front foot with its stout, strong claws. "Please, tell me now. Weren't your names Andrew and Sara?" Her voice sounded as sweet and clear as her song.

"Those *are* our names," said Andrew.

"Those are your old names. Your new names are yet to come," said Mrs. Mole, reaching toward him.

As Andrew bravely reached out to take her paw full of extended claws, he realized he could see everything crystal clear.

"Hey, this is wonderful! I've been in a terrible mess because I lost my glasses. But now I can see!"

"You are seeing by my light, child. I'm afraid when you leave me, you will have trouble with your sight once again. But perhaps it won't be a problem forever."

"You know, of course, Mrs. Mole used to be blind," said Dink, leaning back on his tail and sipping some steaming honey tea.

"Blind! How long ago did this happen? Did you have surgery? Who was your doctor?" asked Sara forgetting her fear. "Maybe he could help Andrew!"

"There, there," Mrs. Mole's voice sounded as gentle as a lullaby. "All events have their moment. First, about your living quarters. I thought you should stay with Rabbit Teleng and his wife Reca. However, Lamper reminded me you are not used to living underground in burrows and holes. So I have asked the rabbits to help you make a proper home. They also will instruct you about the dangers here."

"What dangers?" asked Sara.

"You mean the Snedoms?" asked Andrew. Mrs. Mole nodded her glowing head.

"The Snedoms and their vile leader Krad," said Mrs. Mole. "Teleng will tell you all you need to know. Do pay attention to his words."

"What we really need is to find our way home. I don't even have a change of clothes," said Sara pulling on her torn shirt.

"Everything happens in its time, my child. Now ready yourselves to go to Teleng and Reca's. They will be most gentle," said Mrs. Mole.

Both Andrew and Sara preferred to stay with Mrs. Mole and Dink. Surrounded with her books and glowing light, Mrs. Mole seemed to know everything. And Dink was a great comfort. But before the children could suggest staying, Mrs. Mole called to Dink.

"You'd better go," Mrs. Mole said. "The light will be closed up soon. And I will feel better when you get these two bedded down for a rest."

"Of course, of course. We must avoid that dreadful smoke. Come, chappies. Follow me." Dink hurried to the tunnel entrance, and the children followed him.

"Now, children, remember if you are in danger, you can reach safety by entering one of my tunnels," said Mrs. Mole.

"WHAT DANGER!" boomed Sara. "What's going to happen?"

Mrs. Mole leaned her furry cheek against the top of Sara's head and rubbed Andrew's cheek with her paw. "You must hurry now."

Without another word she gently pushed the children into the dark tunnel behind Dink's soft glowing form. Then Dink scurried quite a distance ahead.

Andrew blinked back tears as he stumbled blindly along in the semi-darkness through the twisting burrow. The palms of his hands began sweating. The moldy smell and the cold dampness of the dirt tunnel rolled over him. Sara panted behind him struggling to keep up. *What am I doing here? Me and my big ideas. How did I get us into this?* thought Andrew.

Finally he saw a strong ray of light coming down the hole from outside. They had made it. Dink leaned back on his tail waiting for them at the tunnel entrance. "We're out in the open now," said Dink. "But we're a bit short on light. Climb on my back, chappies."

Andrew climbed on, snuggling into the comfort of Dink's warm fur and the sound of his hum. "Grab my hand, Sara," said Andrew. He helped her swing up behind him. And they both held on tight as Dink sprang into a darting run.

A pungent smell drifted through the air. A gray, smoky cloud rolled across the floor of the Meadow. The intense, beautiful light faded, giving the Meadow over to shapeless images. The music stopped. The silence seemed deathlike. Everything, but Dink running fast, appeared perfectly still.

"What's happening?" asked Sara. She began coughing from the smoke.

"Just hang on!" said Dink.

Suddenly Dink froze in his path. A silhouette of a winged creature glided above them. Its black shadow fell across the ground covering Dink and the children. Andrew squinted at the shape.

"Sara," whispered Andrew. "What's that?"

"Looks like—"

"It's a Snedom, that demon!" shot back Dink. "Cover your eyes. NOW!"

Both children put their faces down without a question as Dink sprang into a run. Their hearts slammed like jackhammers against their ribs. They dug their fingers deep into Dink's fur and hung on for their lives. The wind whipped at the children as the squirrel sprinted on soundless paws over logs and under brush through the Meadow.

After a long hard run, Dink came to a dead stop. He blinked his black eyes and looked sharply to the left and right. Then he let his hot body sink into the grass. He puffed hard. "Well, that—that was a terrible scare. You're quite safe, of course. We are at Rabbit Teleng's."

"Oh, Dink, you're wonderful!" said Sara. Sliding off his back, she reached up and hugged his neck.

"This is the second time you've saved our lives," said Andrew. "How can we ever thank you?"

"If all goes well, there will be a way, chappie. There will

be a way." And without another word, he left them and darted into the Meadow shadows to hide from the terrible smoke.

TELENG AND RECA RABBIT

ANDREW AND SARA shivered slightly in the smoky dusk. Sara covered her mouth and coughed. Looking around, they could barely make out the tall flowers and grasses. Both children felt dazed and tired after their narrow escape.

"I'm sure hungry," said Andrew.

"My, my, my. We've been expecting you."

The children looked up to see a fluffy brown rabbit peering down at them. In the shadows his body cast a soft glow. He had a nasty red scar over one of his liquid brown eyes. Still, his face appeared gentle.

The rabbit's long ears moved back and forth independently of each other, and his pink nose twitched, moving giant whiskers up and down. He was more than three times as tall as Andrew.

"I am Teleng. Please—come in out of this smoke."

The children followed Teleng into his homey burrow. Family pictures hung on the leaf-covered walls. A large pot of sweet-smelling carrot soup bubbled on an open fire in the center of the room. Eight small beds lined one wall. An extra-long bed, covered with a green and yellow clover quilt, stood against the other wall. A braided pine needle rug spread over the floor. Another brown rabbit sat in a rocker reading in a soft voice to eight plump bunnies—all about Sara's height.

"Please meet Reca, my wife," said Teleng puffing out his chest, "and my dear little ones."

Seeing the visitors, all the brown bunnies tumbled away from their mother and hopped happily around the children. Reca looked at Andrew and Sara with caring mother-eyes. Her long lashes swooped down on her furry cheeks, and she smiled lifting her white whiskers high. Her brown fur glowed, and a peaceful song swirled about her as she hopped towards the children.

"You two are trembling with fatigue. You've had a terrible day. I know you're hungry," said Reca.

"What we really need is to get home," said Sara. "Andrew here is absolutely no help at all! No one seems to take our situation seriously. We don't belong here!"

"Oh, but you do belong here," said Reca, "or you wouldn't be here. What you need now is a little soup in your tummies. Come, come." Without another word she scooped Andrew and Sara up in her arms. She carried them to the large, polished stump that served as the family table. Then she put two steaming acorn bowls of carrot soup in front of them. As the children ate, Teleng and Reca talked in whispered tones.

"I do believe the children should sleep here for the night. We need light before we take them to their own quarters.

Besides, look at their little faces. They're ready to drop," said Reca.

Teleng agreed. "Dark is no time to move them. Can't even breathe in that blasted smoke! I'm sure the Snedoms would love to take their eyes." Teleng rubbed his scar. "That would be quite a prize for Krad."

Reca doubled up four of her bunnies and bedded down Andrew and Sara in two soft, fur-lined beds. Then she picked up a book with a golden cover, settled in her rocker, and began reading again. The children tried hard to listen to the story about Lamper inviting a brave rabbit to his Banquet Hall. But within minutes their heavy eyelids shut, and both fell into an exhausted sleep.

After a long, deep rest, Andrew opened his eyes. Feeling for his cap, he pulled it down hard on his blond head. He looked over at Sara. She stirred and rolled over, sending a tuft of rabbit fur flying from her bed. Baby bunnies tumbled out of their beds.

Wow, I really didn't dream this, he thought. *I AM in a rabbit hole!*

"Ah, our sleepyheads are awake." Teleng's voice sounded deep and musical. "Wash your faces, dear ones. Your porridge is waiting."

Both children, reluctant to leave the warm safety, stumbled out of bed. They joined the bunnies at the family table, and Reca served them each a scoop of steaming sweet potato porridge in their tiny cups. Sara noticed that neither Reca or Teleng were eating.

"Could I get you some?" she asked licking her spoon. "It tastes great."

"Oh, my no," said Reca with a singing voice. "You see, you little ones still must be fed because you haven't been named yet, but Teleng and I eat at Lamper's Banquet table."

"Who is Lamper anyway? We keep hearing his name," asked Sara.

"Lamper is our King. The light of the Meadow comes from him. And everything sings in the warmth of his presence."

"We heard music when we first came here," said Andrew. "Music even from the grass."

"Oh yes, the Meadow usually is in concert—as long as Lamper's light is shining. But then . . ." Reca's whiskers drooped.

"But then there's silence," Teleng said sadly. "Silence while Krad's vulture Snedoms circle and his smoke invades the Meadow."

"Mrs. Mole said you'd tell us about the Snedoms. A Snedom circled us last night, and Dink made us hide our faces. What would've happened if," Sara's voice trembled, "if the Snedom got to us?"

"Eyes!" said Teleng. "They are after your eyes."

He pointed to his red scar. "When I was a young rabbit, I was happily exploring the Meadow." He shook his head. "And I forgot to watch the light. Suddenly, I saw my own long purple shadow in the creeping dark. I began coughing from the smoke. I heard a terrible hiss, and before I could take cover, I saw the enormous black body of a Snedom. It was horrible, horrible," Teleng moaned.

"Down he swooped—his sharp beak sticking out of his purple, naked head. He aimed for my eye—it was all a swirl of horror. As he hung over my face, my nose burned from his stinking hiss. Slicing at me with his beak, he cut through my fur into my flesh."

The hair stood up on the back of Sara's neck. Andrew's eyes widened.

"Blood poured down my face," the rabbit said. "Then the Snedom gripped me with its fearsome black claw and poised to strike me—directly in the eye. If I didn't die, I'd be blinded forever. I knew I was doomed. Then I remembered Lamper's words to me—the words I'd gotten in my training—'Use your song.' I opened my mouth and forced out a few notes. I felt the Snedom release one claw, and I drew in a breath. I sang again. The Snedom let out a wicked hiss and, to my surprise, let me go. Then he lifted his huge body from the ground and flapped away into the dark smoke."

Andrew and Sara stared across the table at Teleng. Sara rubbed the goose bumps on her arms. She remembered the smoke and the circling Snedom and—she shuddered.

"Can't anyone stop them?" asked Andrew.

"They are under Krad's authority, and he's quite brilliant and evil. So far, no one's been able to stop him. I'm afraid he's caused a horrid change in the Meadow." Teleng patted his wife. "All Meadow creatures used to have homes on the Meadow lawn and lived in freedom. Little ones played without a worry. But now we have to live underground and . . ." Teleng's voice trailed off.

"I want facts about this Krad!" said Sara stomping her tiny foot.

"Well, it's a sad tale to tell," Teleng began. "You see, Krad's name—his Meadow name used to be Laho. Long before my birth, Laho lived in Lamper's court. His intelligence and gleaming beauty were well known.

"Oh, yes, they say he was an incredible creature. Wings seven feet across. Golden feathers covered his head and body, and his eyes blazed like two green emeralds from his beautiful face. And could he fly!" said Teleng. "Sometimes he would leave Lamper's court and fly straight up beyond the clouds, then dive down, and soar over the Meadow in an unending dance. He dazzled all who saw him."

Then Reca spoke. "But Laho knew his light came from Lamper's reflection. He began brooding and complaining against Lamper. Soon jealousy ate at Laho's heart. He held secret meetings in the Meadow trying to gather a following. He even said Lamper was dying, and everyone should leave Lamper and let Krad be the leader. Imagine that!" Reca shook her head, letting her long ears flop.

"Why didn't Lamper just kill him?" asked Andrew.

"Well, in a way he did," answered Teleng. "You see, Lamper knew what Laho was up to. He hoped Laho would change his evil ways. Lamper loved Laho deeply. But Laho kept on plotting and lying," said Teleng. "Finally Lamper had had enough.

"One day Laho flew to the grand palace and entered the

Banquet Hall as usual. He sat down to feast and spilled out flattering words of praise to Lamper." Teleng shook his head. "Instead of pleasing the King, the words instantly turned into giant buzzing flies as they left Laho's lying lips. The flies could only make a few pesty circles in Lamper's intense light before dropping dead.

"The great Lamper stood and faced Laho. Everyone in the court fell on their faces. Then Lamper said, 'Your name is no longer Laho, but Krad. And you shall be banished from my light and my court forever.'"

"Wow!" said Andrew in a hushed voice.

"There was a deadly silence." The children stared at the rabbit's serious face as Teleng paused and twitched his whiskers. Then he continued, "When creatures dared to lift their eyes, they were shocked!"

"Why?" asked Sara

"The beautiful Laho had lost his golden splendor. His black looks matched his black heart. He no longer reflected Lamper's light but his own evil. They say he rushed out of Lamper's presence and flew from the palace on sagging wings—screaming curses as he left."

"Where is Krad now?" Sara asked.

"In his cave at the west end of the Meadow. We hear his roaring, but rarely see Krad himself—just those dreadful Snedoms that do his dirty work," said Teleng.

"Yes, he convinced the Snedoms they could make a new, powerful court of light," said Reca. "But all they have been able to do is fill the Meadow with smelly, black smoke. And

Lamper shuts the gates of his kingdom against it, closing in his light."

"Of course, it's during that time the Snedoms leave their roost and fly about looking for eyes," said Dink who had let himself into the rabbit burrow. "If they can blind us, they believe they have stolen our light."

"Oh, Andrew, we've got to get out of here," whispered Sara. "I keep telling you this place is dangerous!"

"I know," said Andrew. He squinted his eyes. *I hate not being able to see. I wish I had my glasses. I know one thing. I have to keep AWAY from Krad and the Snedoms. I can always get more glasses when I get home, but not new eyes!*

THE OLIVE TREE HOUSE

DINK'S GRAY FLUFFY tail stood upright in a huge question mark as he rubbed his paws together by the warm fire.

"Dink! I'm so glad to see you." Sara slipped down from her place at the table and pressed her face into his comforting fur.

"I'm here to help Teleng and Reca get you chaps settled in a wee little home of your own," said Dink.

"But we need to be getting to our real home," said Sara. "Really, Dink. Won't you help us? Settling down in the Meadow is not what I had in mind. I mean, by this time Aunt Janet and Uncle Dave probably think we've been kidnapped. They've probably called the police! We're supposed to be home for supper at six o'clock."

"Actually, they probably haven't missed you, so don't worry," said Reca. "We don't follow a clock here."

"How do you know what time it is then?" asked Sara who was always exact about time and dates.

"We don't live in time. We live in light," answered Teleng. "Come."

39

Sara was about to ask Teleng another question, but the rabbits, their babies, and Dink headed out of the burrow into the Meadow. Sara and Andrew hurried to follow their glow.

Casting its clear sparkle over the Meadow, a golden light greeted them. Yellow buttercups, wild orange poppies, and lavender shooting stars bloomed in glorious patches. The fresh smell of green grass mixed with the scent of honey-suckle and perfumed the air. And every living thing was filled with music. The music sang of celebration. The baby bunnies tumbled among the flowers inviting Sara and Andrew to play hide and seek.

In the joy of it all, the children forgot that Krad and his Snedoms even existed. In the light it seemed unlikely that the danger of dark shadows and thick smoke would threaten them again.

Then Teleng's gentle voice interrupted their laughter. "We must make some arrangements for you children. We have work to do. This way now."

Teleng collected the bunnies and, with Reca and Dink at his side, hopped directly north. The two cousins stopped their play and ran after them.

"Andrew," Sara said as she pulled on the back of his torn shirt, "I don't think they understand that we need to go home. Your folks will be frantic, and I bet they've called my mom. I mean it, Andrew, we're missing children!"

"Don't you think I know that!" Andrew said over his shoulder. "The problem is that the rabbits and Dink don't know where we came from, so how can they help us get home?" He jerked his ragged cap tight on his head as he hurried along.

"Well, Mr. Experimenter, then you'd better get to thinking, 'cause YOU got us into big trouble, and YOU better get us out."

Sara sounded loud and tough, but Andrew could hear her voice trembling.

The group ahead had stopped, and the children caught up with them.

"There." Teleng pointed towards an olive tree with its friendly, spreading branches and green, hard leaves. As they walked closer, they saw gnarled roots exposed above the ground on one side, making a twist of nooks and spaces. "I think this will fill the bill. We can make you quite a nice home here."

The children began exploring the tree roots. They discovered that under the ground was a large flat boulder which had forced the roots up.

"This is a perfect floor!" said Sara, who had gotten into the excitement of things. "Hey, the space is divided into perfect little rooms. This is a great treehouse."

"Come see, chappies, a cellar!" called Dink, who had scrambled under the boulder into a large cave. "Of course! This is good because you can live above ground but can go below for safety."

"Excellent," said Teleng. "Just what I'd hoped for. And this olive tree stands between our home, where you can come for food, and Mrs. Mole's, where you can go for wisdom."

Teleng and Dink helped the children clean out the space.

Dink swept the floor clean with his tail, and Teleng padded it with moss and hung leaves at the doors. Reca unloaded a pine needle basket she'd filled with food from her home. Then she made up two beds, lining each one with tufts of her own brown fur. Dink inverted the cap of a mushroom and filled it with water from the nearby river. It made a fine basin. Teleng hauled in a smooth gray rock to make a table. For a final touch, the bunnies gathered two large flower petals for the children to sit on.

"Come to me, children, we must talk," said Teleng. "As soon as we take the bunnies home, Reca, Dink, and I will join the other named ones at Lamper's Banquet table. We've settled the two of you, but you must remember—when the shadows fall or if you smell smoke, hide yourselves. The Meadow won't be safe. Do not go out until the light returns. Krad's Snedoms will be soaring."

Sara poked Andrew. "Ask him!"

"Ask me what?" asked Teleng.

Sara nervously pulled on a lock of her black hair. "Ah, well—you have been so kind to us, but, well—we want to go back to OUR home. The one we came from."

"Child, I don't know how to find your way home since the Meadow is the only home I know." Teleng reached down and patted Sara's cheek. "If there *is* another home, perhaps Lamper can help you find it."

"Yes, dear ones," said Reca, "if anyone knows how to help, it will be Lamper."

"And just how do we find Lamper?" asked Sara.

"That event will come," said Reca. And before the

cousins could ask anything else, Dink hugged Andrew and Sara good-bye.

"One more thing, chappies. If danger overwhelms you, sing your song."

"What song?" asked Sara.

"The one you were born with, of course," answered Squirrel Dink as he waved his fluffy tail and scurried behind the rabbits. After some distance he stopped and called back, "Take care, pets. Take care!"

The children watched them until they were out of sight. Sara wrinkled her forehead. "And now what'll we do? Our friends are gone. We are only five inches tall, and we have no way to get home." Her green eyes flashed. "If I ever listen to you again, I'll be crazy!" Sara stuck out her bottom lip in a pout and sank to the ground. "You and your big ideas."

"I *have* been trying to think of an idea," said Andrew, "and it seems that this Lamper fellow may be the one with all the answers. This is his Meadow, and if he's the one in charge, I bet he can take care of everything."

"I just want to go home." Sara hid her face in her hands and began to cry.

"For pete's sake! Quit crying," said Andrew sharply. "It won't help anything." Sara looked up and caught Andrew blinking back his own tears.

"It's all right, Andrew." Sara blew her nose. "It's all right to cry. Everyone, even boys, should cry. My brothers do. It's a fact that tears are a release for stress . . . and this is very stressful." She patted Andrew's arm.

Later, as the children sat quietly together in a nook of their olive tree home, they heard soft music all around them.

"Listen—a harp." Sara put her hands against the smooth, gray-green trunk. Andrew put his palms on the wall.

"I can feel the vibrations," he said. The song of the tree filled them with peace and energy. Neither of them moved for a long time.

"You know, Sara, this is a wonderful magical place—this Lamper's Meadow. While we're here, we ought to make the most of it. Come on. Let's go exploring." Andrew unfolded his legs and stood up. "You coming?"

Sara got to her feet and followed Andrew out. Andrew pulled at the bill of his cap and narrowed his blue eyes.

"Sure wish I could see what's around here. Hey, I have an idea." After surveying the olive tree, Andrew stuck the toe of his tennis shoe in a crack in the bark and began to climb.

"Wait for me," said Sara. Being a good tree climber, she scrambled up after him. Neither spoke as they clung to small twigs and felt for toe holds. It was a difficult climb for their small sizes.

Finally Sara called out, "Here's a great seat."

Andrew scooted towards her place on a wide branch that fanned out flat, high above the ground.

"Would you look at that," gasped Sara.

Andrew squeezed his eyes to see. From the top of the olive tree they had a sweeping view. Among the wild oats and swaying grasses, masses of bright, fragrant flowers grew everywhere. Red, blue, and yellow birds sang and flew together in playful patterns. And brown mule deer visited with a sleek bobcat under some blooming trees that bordered the open space.

A large mountain radiant with light stood at the east end of the Meadow. A powerful, crystal-clear river rushed down from the mountain cutting right through the center of the Meadow.

"It looks like a beautiful wild garden," said Sara.

"I wish I could see better," said Andrew. "Look at that mountain!"

"Yeah, it's incredible. I bet there's plenty more to see up there, but the light blocks it out. Andrew! That must be where Lamper lives."

"Then that's where we need to be going," said Andrew. "Into the light." His body shuddered. Suddenly, he felt how small a boy he was. Even if he had been his full height of four feet, eleven inches, he was still a very small boy. And how could he, being such a small boy, approach such a light? He might be completely blinded, or worse. He might be fried!

The two of them sat in the tree seat for a long time. Finally, Sara poked Andrew.

"Well, we can't stay here forever. We'd better make a plan. We definitely need to make a detailed map," said Sara.

"A map! Yeah! That's what we need. But how could we make one? Do you have a pencil or paper?" asked Andrew.

Sara was thinking. Her eyes were closed as she ran her hands through her short black curls. "I've got it!" she said. "Mrs. Mole! She could help us. Her place is full of books—that means pencils, paper, pens—the works. And I bet she's full of detailed facts. Maybe she already has a map of the Meadow."

"Yeah, then with her help we could make our plans and get to Lamper's." Andrew's voice sounded fearless, but he felt his stomach turn over.

THE SHADOWS

THE CHILDREN, INVOLVED in their planning, only now noticed the change creeping over the Meadow. Silence had fallen. Not a bird sang. All music seemed swallowed up by sudden shadows. A chill fell across the children, and Sara's teeth began to chatter.

"How weird," said Andrew, looking over the dark Meadow. "It gives me the creeps."

"It's not like night coming," said Sara. "It's more like . . ." She struggled for words. "Well, like evil."

"Look at that!" Sara pointed east. Something closed across the face of the mountain, shutting the light in.

The flowers closed their petals. The dancing grasses stopped swaying. And the powerful river looked like a long, black snake that vanished down some hole in the dark.

"What's happening?" asked Andrew. "I can't see anything now. But I sure smell smoke." He covered his nose and mouth with his shirt tail. There was a rumble as the ground began to roll and shake.

Sara grabbed for his arm. "Andrew!" Her voice was

breathless. She saw something emerging from the far west end of the Meadow.

"What is it? What?"

"I'm looking—Oh, Andrew . . ." Sara's body turned cold. She dug her fingers into the tree bark as her eyes riveted to something rising out of the ground—it looked like a dark cave. Dense black smoke swirled from the opening and rolled over the Meadow floor.

"There's something terrible way down there," said Sara finding her voice. "I think it might be Kr—Krad!"

A horrible hissing sound and a flapping of huge wings split the silence. As the children looked up, the sky filled with enormous, dark creatures that flew from thorn trees inside the cave.

"Snedoms!" whispered Andrew. "We've gotta get down from here—to our tree cellar." But both children froze as the Snedoms flapped and soared around the sky. They cast monsterlike shadows on the floor of the Meadow. Now a putrid, bitter smell swept up on a wind, burning the children's noses and making their eyes water.

"Phew! Smells like rotten eggs." Andrew wiped his runny eyes with the back of his hand.

By evil magic a figure at the cave entrance seemed to enlarge—to the children's horror. It wore a long, black cloak. A dark hood covered its face.

"It's Krad!" whispered Sara.

With a wild scream Krad flung back the hood with his bony claw. His long, narrow head was bald, and his curled beak looked razor-sharp. His jet-black eyes with glowing yellow centers sliced the dark.

Krad dropped his cloak. Stretching his neck, he peered from side to side. Then he lifted enormous jet-black wings. Spreading open his beak, he broke the dead silence with another piercing screech.

> *Form the night.*
> *Steal the light.*
> *Make them blind,*
> *And they'll be mine!*

"He means us!" said Sara. "Andrew, hurry!"

The children tried to climb down from their place in the tree, but they could only move in slow motion. Their bodies felt like lead.

"Sara, I can't move. I think it's the smell." Andrew's voice fell to a weak whisper. "Whatever that stuff is, we've been gassed."

> *Fly, my Snedoms,*
> *Plunder for the Dark.*
> *There are eyes I know of,*
> *Eyes I've marked!*

Krad's voice rolled like thunder. At his command thousands of Snedoms spread their wings and lifted their awkward bodies into flight.

"Andrew . . ."

Andrew could hardly hear Sara's voice. He turned to see

her lying flat, clinging to a branch. "Crawl! Inch your way along."

"I can't move. I'm falling asleep."

"Sara, come on. Try!"

Then they heard the horrible hissing and felt the wind from the beating wings. A claw slammed down on the branch above them. A shower of broken bark and leaves pelted the children.

"Sara! Your eyes—hide your eyes!" Andrew felt sleep overtaking him.

This is it, thought Andrew, and he buried his head in some olive leaves and rocked in the wind from the mammoth wings flapping above.

"Child, child!" A soft but urgent cooing broke through Andrew's fog. A small, warm body pressed against him. Andrew turned his face and opened his sleepy eyes as wide as he could.

Then the smooth, white bird covered him with her wing, ducked her head beneath it and whispered, "I'm Ceapé, my son. Both of you—on my back. Make no sound."

With all the force that was in him, Andrew moved back across the rough branch to Sara and shook her collapsed body. She stirred, and Andrew shoved her up on Ceapé's waiting back.

"Hold on," Andrew whispered. Then he climbed on behind Sara and wove his fingers into the bird's soft down.

With a rasping shriek, the Snedoms dove to strike.

Ceapé stretched her wings and dropped off the branch. The children's weight made it hard for her to fly. With a racing heart, Ceapé beat her wings hard and flew in close to the ground.

"Drop now!"

The children let go and fell into a thorny blackberry bush. Then tumbling hard, they hit rocky ground. Ceapé, free of her precious burden, darted up into the open smoky sky. And the Snedoms gave chase.

"Hurry!" Sara gained her footing first and pulled Andrew up. "Run! Run! We've gotta find a tunnel."

Andrew reached for his cap, but it was gone. And now was not the time to search for it.

The children heard the sound of faint cooing mixing with horrible hissing and powerful flapping. Their lungs hurt as they ran hard. The friendly flowers and stands of grass now seemed like a frightening jungle in the smoke. They kept struggling through the maze until Sara finally found a mound of dirt.

Oh, please let this be a tunnel, she thought dropping to her knees. "Here! Dig here!"

Andrew fell beside her and began digging through wet grass roots. Sharp rocks cut their hands as they piled the heavy lumps of dirt aside.

Suddenly, a thin cry pierced the sky. The children stopped their digging. A screeching hiss filled their ears.

"Ceapé! They've got Ceapé," cried Sara.

"Don't stop! Dig!" Andrew's voice cracked.

Finally, there was a hole. They slipped through into a cold, hard dirt tunnel below. Both were panting and shaking. Andrew felt for his cousin. They sank to the ground, holding on to each other. The dank earth smell and darkness settled over them.

"Do you think—the nasty Snedoms—? Oh . . ."

Sara began to weep softly. Tears filled Andrew's eyes and spilled down his dirty cheeks.

"If they hurt Ceapé—if they tore out her eyes, I'll—I'll KILL them!" cried Sara.

"They might've killed her!" Andrew doubled up his fist. "She saved our lives. If she's still alive, we've gotta find her. She'll need help. First let's try and find Mrs. Mole. If this is one of her tunnels, we'll find her if we just keep walking."

The children joined hands and began feeling their way along the dark, narrow, dirt hall.

"Watch it. There's a root sticking up," said Sara. "Hey, it feels like we're turning."

The children shuffled along the pitch-black burrow, sometimes reaching for each other, other times feeling for the cold damp wall. It seemed to them as if they had been groping in the dark for hours.

"Someone's in here." Sara came to a dead stop, and Andrew ran into her. "Andrew, someone's here," she moaned. "I can feel it. What'll we do?"

Andrew grabbed Sara's arm, and they both stood dead still—listening.

"Hear that?" asked Andrew. "What—what is it?"

"Sounds like a—a snore," whispered Sara.

"Well, whatever it is, don't wake it up!" said Andrew. "Just stand still, and let me think. I wish I knew where we were."

"We sure can't go back. There's only a dead end behind us and Snedoms outside the hole." Sara pulled on Andrew's arm. "Think we'd better try going on ahead. Mrs. Mole can't be too far away. We've already walked for miles. If this thing grabs us, scream bloody murder, and maybe Mrs. Mole will hear us."

"O.K., but quiet—don't even breathe. Maybe we can get by it."

Andrew led the way in complete silence, walking Indian-style on his toes, the way he used to in the woods behind his house. Sara fell in behind him, hoping her heart knocking in her rib cage wouldn't wake the creature. Andrew's hands were wet with sweat, and he wiped them on the back of his pants. He knew this might be it.

The snores grew louder as they walked. The children pressed against the wall. Andrew stuck out his hand in the pitch black to feel his way.

"Ugh—horrible, horrible!!" He yelled and pulled his hand to his chest as if he'd been burned.

"What—"

"Th—there . . . there. It's right there. It's cold and sticky. Oh, horrible!" Andrew began trembling, and Sara grabbed his shirt with both hands.

The dark seemed to be taken over by the creature, and its whole presence blocked the burrow in front of them. Before the children could move, the creature opened one huge, golden glowing eye and, with a snap, shot out its long sticky tongue, whipped it about the two of them, and jerked them to its mouth. The children screamed. Surprised, it let out a deafening croak and dropped them in the dirt.

"Wakin' a toad from a sound sleep is a bad idea. You rascally kids oughtta know that." Godo opened both huge eyes and gave a lazy blink. I'm Toad Godo. I've been down here waitin' for ya."

Sara rubbed her bruises. "Well, you weren't very polite. You nearly scared us to death."

"Sorry, missy. It's just a reaction from my past. It's a sad tale to tell, but I used to have to eat like that. Since I've been named, that's all behind me."

"You say you've been waiting for us?" asked Andrew.

"Oh, yeah. Mrs. Mole knew you kids were in trouble and needed help. I'm supposed to get ya on down to her place."

"Well, we *are* glad to have you help us. You just took us by surprise," said Sara.

"Sure, sorry about that snorin'. I just took a little snooze waitin' for ya. Never know when a toad might need extra energy for a battle or somethin'."

Somehow Godo turned himself around in the tunnel, sat quietly for a second, and began to glow. Now the children could see Godo's dark green, lumpy body filling the tunnel space from side to side. Then he moved forward with a short hop.

"Better not touch him or we'll get warts," said Andrew in a hushed voice.

"Don't be ridiculous," snapped Sara. "It's a fact that those lumps are just glands." She felt brave, having found out the "monster" was actually a friend. "Listen!" said Sara tilting her head. "He sounds like a banjo."

"Yeah, must be Godo's music," said Andrew.

Both children walked behind Godo, letting waves of relief wash over them. The cheerful music and the light from a friend filled them with hope—hope that they would eventually find their way to safety.

THE CHOICE

AFTER A FEW bends in the tunnel, the children saw a bright light ahead and they heard sweet strains of a familiar song.

"Mrs. Mole?"

"Right you are, missy," answered Godo. "And I bet you'll find some honey tea to fix ya up."

As they entered the chamber, Mrs. Mole opened her arms. Sara and Andrew ran to her, burying their faces in her velvet fur. She gently patted them.

"There, there. You've had an awful time. But you're safe with me now. Do a little crying. It's good for the brave to cry. And you've been exceedingly brave children."

Tears began streaming down Sara's grimy cheeks, and in a moment Andrew let his tears come too. Mrs. Mole pulled a great handkerchief from her yellow apron pocket and wiped their eyes.

"Now blow," she said in a motherly voice. "Godo, you did good work." Mrs. Mole smiled at the toad. "Please, refresh yourself with some honey tea."

"I'm afraid I nearly scared the kids to death," said Godo

pouring himself some tea into a walnut shell. "Folks tell me my snorin' makes quite a racket. But it never bothers me!"

"The burrow was pitch dark for the children," said Mrs. Mole. "And your glow breaking through rescued them. I do thank you." Godo puffed out his great toad chest.

The children's eyelids began to droop. *My legs feel really weak*, thought Andrew. And seeing Sara stretch and yawn, he yawned in response. *Oh rats, I don't want to fall asleep now. Mrs. Mole's so bright, I can see EVERYTHING.* Too tired to fight his fatigue, Andrew gave in to his weary body and sat down, letting his head rest on his arms.

After a long sleep, Andrew stirred, pulled the soft blanket off his head, and then came instantly awake. He sat up. Looking around, he saw Sara sleeping in a small, fur-lined bed beside him. Mrs. Mole sat before the fire taking something (he couldn't tell what) from the air and spinning it into yarn. Her spinning wheel seemed to sing.

"Nice sleep? I hope you enjoyed the bed I put you in," she said without turning her head. Memories of what had happened flooded his mind, and he shook his head hard to clear his brain.

"Come here, my child." Mrs. Mole stopped her spinning to pour Andrew a steaming cup of honey tea.

He sat at her feet and took the warm blue cup in both hands, smelling the sweet smell of honey. It reminded him of the honey and peanut butter sandwiches his mother made for him, and tears sprang to his eyes.

"There, there. Drink your tea." Mrs. Mole continued her

spinning as Andrew sipped. As soon as the tea reached his stomach, he began to feel clear-headed and strong.

"Oh, Mrs. Mole, we had the most terrible time. That black, horrible Krad came up out of the ground. And if it weren't for Ceapé, his Snedoms would have gotten us."

Still sleepy-eyed, Sara had slipped out of her bed and curled up by Andrew. "Please, do you know anything about dear Ceapé?" she asked.

"Yes, yes I do." Mrs. Mole stopped her work and handed Sara some tea. "After Ceapé flew with you from the tree and dropped you to the ground, she darted up so the Snedoms would chase her."

"Oh, I know it was to pull 'em off our trail. We heard a terrible cry, as if she were being—tortured." Andrew ducked his head and stared into his cup.

"What happened to her?" asked Sara. "Don't spare us the facts. If those Snedoms—"

"She's been blinded." Mrs. Mole interrupted Sara. "We'd hoped this sort of thing would never happen again. We've learned to take care when the dark smoke smothers the Meadow." Mrs. Mole lowered her eyes and shook her head. "But Ceapé threw caution away when she flew to help you."

"Blind! This is absolutely the very worst!" said Andrew. Straining to see without his glasses was hard, but the thought of total darkness forever was crushing.

"What can we do for Ceapé?" asked Sara.

"We can kill Snedoms!" yelled Andrew. "Let me at 'em!" He jumped to his feet and put up his fists.

"Andrew, you're not a fighter," said Sara pulling on his pant leg.

"There are some things worth fighting for, Sara. Everyone must choose just which things those are," said Mrs. Mole. "But, Andrew, Snedoms are only soldiers. Krad is the general."

"Then it's Krad I'm going to get!"

"Krad is a strong enemy, my son. No one could meet Krad without much preparation. He is evil. Very EVIL." For a moment the spinning wheel stopped and, gazing into space, Mrs. Mole sighed. Her song was gone. Then she began working again.

Andrew stood still watching her glowing form.

"How would I prepare to—to fight Krad? I mean, what should I learn? Who could teach me?"

"I myself will prepare you," said Mrs. Mole solemnly.

"You?" Andrew looked at Mrs. Mole's long eyelashes and yellow calico apron. "Please excuse me for saying this—but you—you're a girl, and girls don't go to battle."

"See how much you have to learn, my son? The battle against the Dark is a battle for anyone who is prepared."

"Well, maybe I should be prepared, too, then. If Ceapé was so brave for us, I can learn to be brave," said Sara.

"It's more than learning to be brave, my child. It is wise to fear the power of evil," said Mrs. Mole. "To be prepared you must wear armor and learn how to use the sword. But most important of all, you need to learn how to set your mind like steel against Krad's mind. He's brilliantly vile. And given half a chance, he'll hypnotize you with sweet words of hidden evil."

Sara and Andrew sat at Mrs. Mole's feet. Both were silent—thinking about the danger they were agreeing to face—a danger that could *kill* them.

"Well?" asked Mrs. Mole after some time. "Are you ready to put yourself in training?"

"I would like—well, some more facts," said Sara. Her green eyes peered up into Mrs. Mole's bright black eyes. "It seems to me we'd be real foolish to tackle Krad unless we're sure this armor would work."

"Excellent statement, my daughter. Indeed the armor will be made to suit each of you." Mrs. Mole rocked the treadle of her spinning wheel. "And the sword has already been forged and tested. It's the finest ever crafted." Stopping her work, Mrs. Mole looked Sara full in the face. "And I will teach you the secrets of the Named Ones."

"Secrets!" Andrew shot his hands into the air. "Tell us now!"

"I can only teach you if you find it in your hearts to agree to the training." Mrs. Mole twitched her short, white whiskers. "Don't be hasty with your decision. Once you enter in, I will expect a great deal from you."

"Like what?" asked Sara twisting the torn front of her blouse.

"You must put your trust in me. I will expect you to work extremely hard. And once the training is over—once you are prepared—"

"You'll expect us to meet Krad!" Andrew said with a

shout. "And meet him we will! Eyeball to eyeball!" Andrew began shadow boxing around the room.

Sara shuddered. She felt she understood the danger better than her younger cousin. She had a feeling that this decision was more important than either of them realized.

"I think there are some things we don't understand," said Sara.

"Even if I explained the secrets, you could not understand them yet. You must ask your heart if you should step into training." Mrs. Mole sounded mysterious. "If your answer is yes, then you will be taught—everything."

"I don't need to think about it," said Andrew. "I'm ready to start now!"

Mrs. Mole nodded in agreement. "And you, my daughter?"

"Ah . . . I don't know." Sara scuffed the toe of her tennis shoe on the floor. "Well, I guess so."

"That will never do. You must have a knowing in your heart to put faith into anything. Even if your faith is tested in the middle, you must start with faith at the beginning to come out with faith at the end.

"Come with me, my son. We will begin at once." Mrs. Mole stood and took Andrew by her stout claws and led him towards a tunnel.

"Are you just going to leave me here?" asked Sara.

"You'll be safe. Just rest and think," said Mrs. Mole.

Sara's lower lip stuck out in a pout, and she flopped onto the floor. "All I wanted was more facts. Is that too much to ask?"

Mrs. Mole smiled. "Facts lead you to faith, but your heart takes you in."

ANDREW'S TRAINING

UPRIGHT ON HER back feet, Mrs. Mole shuffled through the narrow tunnel. Her pear-shaped body glowed like a light bulb.

"I feel bad leaving Sara behind. Couldn't she just come and watch?" Andrew realized that since coming to Lamper's Meadow, he and Sara had been through everything together.

"She cannot watch your training unless she is in training herself. And that's her decision. Besides, she would drain your concentration. We are strict about this." Mrs. Mole made a quick turn to the right and entered a room. Andrew followed. A door shut softly behind them.

The large room, brightly lit by Mrs. Mole, was perfectly round. And a seamless mirror completely covered the walls, ceiling, and floor.

Andrew gasped. His matted, dirty blond hair stood in peaks, and his cheeks were smudged with dirt. His torn, filthy shirt and jeans hung on his frame. He looked like a forlorn scarecrow.

"Look at me! My clothes are like the rags my dad uses in

the garage." Wiping his forehead with the palm of his hand, he smeared the grime across his face.

"I'm so dirty." He became aware that he looked small and skinny. Everywhere he turned, he saw another discouraging view of himself. He felt embarrassed to think that moments ago he had punched the air with his tight fist and promised to fight the evil Krad. Andrew put both hands over his eyes.

"It is hard to see yourself, really see yourself, at the beginning of training, but that's where we all start." Mrs. Mole's musical voice had changed, and the change shocked Andrew into peeking out.

She stood in the middle of the room, her eyes closed. Her voice was deep and seemed to echo when she spoke. "While you are in training, you will call me Wimdos, for that is my true name—the name given to me by Lamper. My name shall be your first secret."

"Wimdos . . . Wimdos. Oh, Mrs. Mole, I mean, Wimdos, I'm not sure I can go into training. I mean—ah— look at me. I'm a real mess and—"

"And feeling too weak and small to take on Krad? Oh, yes, I know you do. If you were not aware of your weakness, you'd rely on yourself and not on the Truth."

"That *is* the truth," said Andrew pointing at his reflection. "Just look at me." He tried to swallow the lump in his throat.

"Come to me," said Wimdos with great authority. "Kneel and answer these questions set before you!"

Andrew stumbled towards Wimdos. Her eyes looked like two burning coals. Trembling, he knelt in front of her.

"Do you promise to pledge yourself to the Truth and go into training as Lamper's son of light?"

From somewhere deep within, Andrew felt a surge of electricity rush through his body. "I do promise!"

Reaching down deep into an apron pocket, Wimdos drew out a diamond sword from which streamed pure rays of light. Brilliant rubies, emeralds, and pearls adorned the handle, and the dazzling colors reflected in the mirrors over and over.

Wimdos rested the blade heavily on Andrew's right shoulder, then on the left, and finally on his head. Andrew smelled the scent of cedar and pine breaking over him. "By Lamper's sword of Truth, I call you into training!"

What felt like a bolt of lightning ran through Andrew. His body buckled, and he slumped over on the mirrored floor. As he lay on the floor face down unable to move, he felt the sensation of needles jabbing him in his head. He tried to cry out, but the sound stuck in his throat. Finally, the pain stopped. A swirling, warm breeze soothed him from the top of his head to his chin.

Tears leaked out as Andrew slowly opened his eyes. Looking back at him from the mirrored floor, Andrew saw himself. Pulling up to his knees, he touched his reflection. His hair, shining like gold, lay softly around his clean face. And his eyes were a blazing blue.

"What's happened to me?" whispered Andrew. "Look—" He pulled his fingers gently down his cheek. "I'm clean."

Wimdos laid her cheek on top of Andrew's head. "Cleaning is painful."

Then Andrew noticed his hands were dirty, and his clothes were still tattered. "I don't understand."

"You are just beginning. Now we must train your mind. Long before you battle Krad, you must do battle with your own mind. You have been given the power to reach the unseen, but it is up to you to control your thinking." Andrew dropped his head.

"You are a dreamer. Your world needs dreamers, my son. Dreamers are inventors. But there is a time to dream and a time to stop dreaming. Are you ready?"

Andrew raised his chin and looked at Wimdos's burning eyes. "I'll try."

"Excellent. Sit before me. Close your eyes. Now, my son, I want you to see a picture—a picture of me in your mind. See my body, my eyes, my whiskers, my light."

"Yeah, I can see you. It's sort of like daydreaming."

"Now, focus on the picture. Do not let your mind drift off into space. Hold a picture of me in Lamper's light."

Andrew sat cross-legged on the floor in front of Wimdos with his eyes shut tight. He saw the outline of her body. Her black eyes were burning, and the light poured from her like the sun on an early summer morning. *Hmmm . . . summer morning. I love summer mornings*, he thought.

His thoughts began to roll along. He saw his mother making pancakes in her bright yellow kitchen. He watched her pour a glass of milk for him at his place at the table. Smells of warm maple syrup and melted butter made his stomach growl. *Boy, am I hungry. I wonder if I'm gonna get to eat soon.* Pictures of hamburgers and french fries with a pile of red catsup floated through his thoughts.

"Andrew, concentrate!" Wimdos spoke sharply.

Andrew opened his eyes. Wimdos had not moved. She stood glowing, her feet firmly fixed on the mirrored floor.

"Try again. Mastering this task takes practice. But until you can control your mind, I can't disclose many secrets to you. Begin again."

Closing his eyes, Andrew focused on the picture of Wimdos. Her image was sharp in his thoughts. He watched as her whiskers moved up and down, and he started to look into her eyes when he thought about his glasses. He saw them lying on the floor of Mr. Maxwell's basement. *I hope no one steps on them. Golly, I gotta find them as soon as I get home, or else I'm gonna be in terrible trouble.* He seemed to see the glasses lift off the floor and fly around the basement. In his daydream Andrew began running with his hands in the air grabbing after them.

"Andrew." The voice of Wimdos cut through the daydream and jerked him back to her form of light. He saw her again in his mind. "Good, my son. Now concentrate on the light I am pointing to."

Andrew could see Wimdos fading and a blinding light taking shape. "Concentrate because Lamper wants to speak with you. His voice comes from the light. Ready?"

"I think so."

"Then focus on him and collect the words he's sending to you."

Andrew sat motionless letting the picture of light fill his mind. A still, quiet voice began to speak.

I love you, son of light. You listen well, my child. Listening will bring you my wisdom.

Andrew thought back, *Will you be with me when I fight Kr—Krad?*

Indeed, I will—if you will listen for my voice, I can tell you what to do. Learn to rule your mind.

Andrew's eyes flew open.

"Wimdos, I'm afraid—"

"Don't be afraid." Wimdos laid her velvet cheek against Andrew's forehead. "Lamper will always be with you."

Wimdos helped Andrew practice listening to Lamper for some time. Then Wimdos said, "Fine work, my little one. You are learning the art of listening, and I am very proud of you. You must practice this often. It is difficult to master daydreams. They like to take over our minds like runaway horses. If wandering thoughts take your mind, you won't hear Lamper speak. Practice wherever you happen to be—at Teleng's burrow, your treehouse, in the Meadow. You will soon learn you can be linked together always with Lamper. Whatever you do, never think into emptiness. Concentrate on Lamper's light."

Andrew peered at the glowing Wimdos. Indeed, he had heard Lamper's voice in his mind as clearly as if he had spoken out loud. *I remember hearing voices in my mind before*, he thought. *Like the time I rode my bike to Lemon Grove Park and nearly got hit by that motorcycle. It was Dad's voice that shouted, "WATCH WHERE YOU'RE GOING!" And Dad wasn't even there. And I'm always hearing Mom say, "Did you brush your teeth?" after I've gotten in bed. It'll be good to hear Lamper's voice—especially since,* Andrew's whole body shuddered, *I promised to fight Krad.*

"Now, my son, I must ready you for the sword. Hold out your hands."

Andrew looked at his grubby hands and wiped them hard on his pants. To his surprise his hands got dirtier the more he rubbed them. They even began to let off an awful smell, like the bait he'd once forgotten for a week in his fishing box.

"Ick! This is terrible!" He stuck his arms straight out in order to try to get away from the smell. "I can't stand it!"

"Give me your hands!" said Wimdos firmly. Andrew stuck his hands in front of him and turned his head. The smell made him feel like throwing up.

Wimdos took his hands in her powerful broad paws and gripped her claws together. A searing pain shot through Andrew's fingers and up his arms. Wimdos held on tight. Reeling in pain, he tried to jerk his arms free.

"Let go!" he screamed. "You're killing me!"

Wimdos didn't move or speak. She held Andrew fast. Shaking, Andrew fell to his knees. Finally, the pain began to ease.

The foul smell vanished, and the wonderful scent of pine and cedar again filled the cavern. As the blood rushed back to his fingertips, Andrew's hands tingled. Then the same soothing warmth that had bathed his head washed over his hands and up his arms. Wimdos gently dropped his hands.

Andrew opened his eyes and looked at the back of his hands. Completely clean, his hands seemed to have a glow all their own. He turned them over. His palms felt strong.

"I am so sorry this hurts you. But there is no other way for any of us. Everyone who is cleansed goes through pain when he is washed. You see, you are being washed inside and out. Lamper will always be here for your comfort and help."

Andrew blinked his eyes hard to clear the tears away.

"I know you hated seeing how dirty you were. But that is behind you now. You are becoming new." Wimdos knew there would be more cleaning, but that was in the future.

"You are ready for the sword of Truth," said Wimdos. Reaching down into her apron pocket, she drew out the incredible shining sword. "This is Ritips."

Raising the sword above her head, she swung, cutting the air with the sword's piercing light.

"It is Lamper whom you serve." The voice of Ritips rang out strong and clear. Wimdos passed the sword over Andrew's head.

"And He is before all things, and in Him all things hold together."[1]

Still on his knees, Andrew now fell on the floor and covered his eyes.

"Stand, my son. Do not be afraid of the Truth. The Truth has come to strengthen you and set you free. Now take the sword."

Andrew's hands began to tingle again. He felt the energy flow to his arms. Standing up, he reached out his right hand

and took Ritips from Wimdos. To his surprise the sword shortened its length to fit him.

"It feels light!" Gripping the jeweled hilt, he lifted Ritips high and cut through the air.

"Believe in the light, in order that you may become sons of light."²

Andrew slashed the space in front of him.

"I have come as light into the world, that everyone who believes in Me may not remain in darkness."³

The sword seemed to have a life of its own as it spoke.

"Now that you have the feel of it, I want to instruct you. Ritips exists to battle Krad and all the enemies of the light. You must learn to battle from power and strength, not fear and weakness. And this is a state of the heart and mind. You must remain under my discipline and teaching."

Remembering the horrible Krad and his hideous Snedoms made Andrew shudder. How could he keep from being afraid?

"I understand your fear, my son, but remember your secrets. If you rule your thoughts, you can hear Lamper's voice, and he can guide you. And the sword can battle evil in the hands of a son or daughter of light. The fact is, we of Lamper's Meadow have been waiting for you for a long time." Wimdos paused.

Andrew held the sword with both his hands and looked Wimdos full in her furry, radiant face.

"What do you mean, 'waiting for me'?" he asked.

"When we saw the two of you, we knew."

"Knew what?" Andrew moved very close to Wimdos.

Only the sword was between them. She put her claws on top of his hands.

"You will see and know for yourself, my son. But now we must stop talking. I must train you to use the sword."

Then the orders began to roll out. "Face the mirrors. Plant your feet. Get your bearings. Stay light on your feet. Watch your posture . . ." Shining Ritips was becoming Andrew's friend.

SARA EXPLORES

SARA SAT AND sulked for a long while after Andrew left with Mrs. Mole. *It's really dumb of Andrew to rush into training. It's dangerous business—risking blindness or worse—his LIFE—to fight that stupid Krad,* thought Sara. *Anyway, it's not any of our business what they do here. We just need to make a map, find this Lamper, and go home.*

Sara pulled her knees to her chest and wrapped her arms around her legs. *I think it's time I took over and made plans. Andrew's just too hot-headed. No telling how long he's gonna be off with Mrs. Mole. Hmmmm . . .*

Sara got up from her spot by the fireplace. "Maybe I could find some paper and a pen. That's one reason we came here in the first place, to get stuff to make a map."

Wandering around the room, Sara stopped at the spinning wheel. "I wonder what she's making on this, and what she makes it from." Sara lightly touched the great wheel. "Ouch!" She jerked her hand back and poked burning fingers into her mouth. "What in the world?"

Examining the frame, she found nothing that should cause a burn. Ripping off a piece of her torn blouse, she touched the wheel with the cloth. Now the whole spinning wheel turned red hot. In seconds the material burst into flames and fell at her feet.

"Oh no, I'm gonna catch the whole place on fire," she said stomping on the flames. The spinning wheel began to cool off.

Frightened, Sara backed off and started her search for some paper. This time she avoided touching anything of Mrs. Mole's. Looking in some cupboards, she saw tiny blue cups and plates but nothing to help her make a map. She searched the books on the shelves that lined the walls. *Maybe I'll find a map of the Meadow somewhere*, she thought as she thumbed through the first book.

Suddenly she heard a soft singing voice. *"A gentle answer turns away wrath."*[4]

"Who's there?" Sara dropped the book. Her green eyes narrowed and roved around the room, looking for the unexpected visitor. "I said, who's there? Answer me at once!" Her voice sounded strong, but her legs felt like rubber. Without Mrs. Mole, the room was dim. Only a small hole in the top of the burrow and two small flickering candles offered some light. Sara strained to see.

I must be losing my mind. I'm hearing things. Sara picked up the book again. Rubbing her hands over the smooth, musty leather cover, she felt her hands tingle. She opened the book. Again the sweet voice filled the air.

"Do not let kindness and truth leave you."[5]

This time she noticed the smell of pine and cedar in the room.

"Wha—what's going on here?" she whispered. She closed the book and opened it gently to another page.

The voice spoke again. *"The wise listen to advice."*[6]

"You're incredible, little book." She reached down and kissed its cover. Flipping from page to page, she listened to the beautiful voice instruct her.

"A joyful heart is good medicine, but a broken spirit dries up the bones."[7]

"Do all you books speak?" asked Sara. She held onto her special find while pulling another book from the shelf. It seemed as if the pages were glued together. "Hmmm . . . why won't you open?"

She tried another and another. Not one would give way. "What a strange library!" She reopened her first book.

"Like a bird that wanders from her nest, so is a man who wanders from his home . . . Do not forsake your own friend."[8]

"Ceapé! Is that what you're trying to tell me, little book? Oh, dear Ceapé! Here I'm thinking of maps when I should be searching for her."

Sara put the book back on the shelf. Getting a candle from the mantle, she walked by its patch of light down the narrow hall, looking for the way out to the Meadow.

Trudging along the dirt path, she shivered as she wondered if all of Mrs. Mole's books would speak if she could open them. What a strange place—this Lamper's Meadow.

"Oh, Andrew, I miss you." Her words rolled down the tunnel echoing her loneliness.

After walking a long while, she saw a huge mound of dirt

blocking her path. Stopping and holding the candle above her head, she squinted her eyes in the poor light.

"Well, I'll just climb over—Ohhh!" The dirt moved, and two yellow eyes centered with black diamonds raised up and blinked. "Godo!"

"Well, missy, just where you goin' by yourself?" Godo lifted his chin above the dirt and studied Sara.

"It's about time for me to do something around here! I need to find Ceapé! Mrs. Mole told us she's—" Sara's voice broke with sadness, "blind. Blind from those terrible Snedoms. If it hadn't been for Ceapé, I don't know what would have happened to us."

"And so you're gonna find her?"

"That's part of my plan."

"Well, kid, how about you tellin' me," said Godo rolling his big eyes, "the rest of your plan." He lowered his mouth back down into the mud.

"I'm gonna make a map. No one is doing one thing about getting us home again. It seems to me this Lamper could help us, but I have no idea how to get to him." Sara's words tumbled out. "Andrew and I saw his light from high in the olive tree. But down on the ground everything looks different."

Godo squeezed his eyes into yellow slits. "And do ya have a plan to protect yourself?"

Sara stomped her foot. "Of course, I do, Godo. I wouldn't go off without a plan—especially after our last mess with the Snedoms. I'm smarter than that. I figure I'll be in the Meadow only during the light. That way I'll be safe. And if

I make a map as I go, it'll be a cinch to find my way back. Besides, I can hide in the treehouse. I couldn't find paper or pencils, but I can use tree bark to write on and a piece of chalky rock to draw with. You see, you don't need to worry 'cause I've thought of everything." Sara felt proud of herself for all the plans she had made.

"Missy, you've not thought of everythin', but I can tell by the set of your jaw, you're goin'. I suppose the only way I could keep ya here is to tie ya up with my tongue. Ya sure don't know enough to go strollin' about the Meadow alone."

"I DO know enough!" Sara hated anyone to question her knowledge. Pulling herself up to her full nearly five inches of height, she put her hands on her hips. "Well, are you gonna let me go or not?"

"It's against my better judgment. But you're sure determined. Remember, kid, you do have power to—"

"Of course, I do," interrupted Sara as she started her climb up and over Godo's buried body. She could feel the vibration of his banjo music under her feet.

"Ick, this is really muddy!" Her feet sank and stuck. She pulled them hard. "Oh, now I've lost my shoes. Rats and double rats!!"

Trying to hold the candle and search in the sloppy mud for her shoes put her off balance, and she started sliding down Godo's back. In her fall she flung the candle to the right, and she fell to the left. Picking herself up, she let out a yell.

"I'm covered with this blasted mud! Godo, help me!" But

Godo only shook the walls of the tunnel with his snoring. "Some friend you are!" she muttered .

Wiping herself off as best she could, Sara pulled her muddy socks off and left them. Walking on bare tiptoes, she felt her way in the dark down the cold, damp dirt path. After making the next turn, she saw light. *Oh, thank goodness*, she thought as she scrambled into the tunnel opening.

Breathing in the fresh air and standing in the beautiful light, Sara felt refreshed. Bright blue lupin bobbed in the sweet-smelling breeze above her head. The music of wood-winds played a tune coaxing her to dance. Before she thought about it, she began twirling and skipping to the music through the tall grasses and radiant flowers. The ground was alive under her bare feet—alive with color and sound. The whole Meadow seemed to bow and sway and sing with Sara in joyful celebration.

Finally, she collapsed under a white violet to catch her breath. The song of a yellow-breasted meadowlark floated through the air, and she was about to lean back and rest when she remembered. *What am I doing? I gotta look for Ceapé.*

Knowing she must not lose her way, Sara dug about the ground until she found a small white rock. *Great! This will work.* She picked up a fragment of eucalyptus bark. "Perfect!" Using the rock, she marked the tunnel entrance on the bark to start her map.

Spying a hard-packed trail that looked well-traveled, she followed it, marking her map as she went. As she walked, thoughts of Ceapé filled her mind. She decided when she found her dear friend, she would bring her back to Mrs.

Mole's. Ceapé would have tender care there even after she and Andrew went home.

"And just who is YOU?"

Sara had been walking fast with her head down in thought. Now she snapped to attention at the sound of the demanding voice.

"I—I'm Sara Katherine Stevens. And who are you?" she asked timidly.

The creature towered in front of her. The blunt snout and prominent nostrils looked odd on the small head. "I be Gered and this, girly, is MY territory." The Gered exposed her large teeth and suddenly flared out her quills. She slapped her fat, quilled tail to and fro.

"Ah, ahh, well, is Gered your Meadow name?" asked Sara.

"I don't want no Meadow name, thank ya very much. I named myself. I'm independent, and I likes it that way." Gered waddled about Sara waving her terrible tail.

"Did ya eat anything in my territory?" Gered's small black eyes had a greedy look. And Sara noticed there was no music coming from her.

"No, ma'am." Sara decided she should be extremely polite to Gered. "But I am real hungry. Maybe you would be so kind as to help me find something to eat."

"Deed I will not! Didn't ya hear me? Or is ya deaf? This be MY territory. The food here be MINE. And I ain't no fool to give any to the likes of you!" Gered slapped her tail hard on the ground.

"Excuse me, but don't you eat at Lamper's Banquet table like the others who live here?"

"That, Miss Nosy, be my business. I has all I needs to eat right here with my beechnuts and acorns, that is, if nobody gits in here to steal my food." Gered waddled closer to Sara to get a better look. Leaning down, she squinted hard. "My eyesight's some bad. Say, girly, you're just a bit of a thing," she growled.

Sara pulled back from Gered's frightening form and terrible breath. *Oh, brother, am I in trouble now. I hope I can talk my way out of this and away from her!*

Sara took in a shivering breath and started talking as fast as she could.

"Well, I am NOT interested in stealing beechnuts and acorns. Really I'm not! I eat things like chicken noodle soup and hot dogs and popcorn. I'm really just trying to find the bird Ceapé. She saved my life. Now, you see, it's my turn to help her. Mrs. Mole told me that she's been . . . been blinded by the dreadful Snedoms and—"

"Take my advice, Miss Nosy," interrupted Gered. "Stay out of it! Ceapé got herself in trouble. She can just git herself out of trouble. You go stake some territory and mind your own business. Ya can't never git ahead unless you looks out for yourself."

Sara looked at Gered. Her gnawing teeth, gruff growl, and quills—it was odd, but Sara felt a little sorry for her. Perhaps it was because Gered had no music. But she wouldn't be foolish. If she could just leave, she'd mark this territory on her map and stay out of Gered's way.

"Ah, well, I guess I'll be going. Sorry I troubled you," said Sara.

"Not gonna listen, is you, girly? Well, it's your funeral, but if ya ask me, ya oughtta mind your own business. Goodbye then, and good riddance." Sticking her snout in the dirt, Gered rambled down the path away from Sara. Then she lifted her head and yelled back. "Oh, yeah, ya can find that bird at the end of my territory. I pushed her out—straight down the path there."

Sara raced down the path. Then from a safe distance she yelled at Gered, "You greedy, mean creature! How could you be so hard-hearted!"

SARA AND CEAPÉ

THE PATH MADE a double twist through the woods and ended in a wide clearing. From where she stood, Sara could hear the music of the mighty river, but she couldn't see the water. If Gered had told the truth, Ceapé was close by . . . if nothing had happened to her in the meantime.

Leaving the path, Sara sat on a rock to rest and marked her map. Wiping the sweat from her forehead, she decided it was time to watch for the long purple shadows that had overtaken her and Andrew once before.

Then the sweet voice from Mrs. Mole's book filled her mind. *"Like a bird that wanders from her nest, so is a man who wanders from his home . . . Do not forsake your own friend."*[8]

Standing on a rock, she called out, "Ceapé, can you hear me? I gotta find you, my dear friend. Ceapé!" She yelled again and again. But there was no answer. There was no music. Sara trembled. She felt afraid, like she did sometimes back home when her father made her feed the dog at night in the dark backyard. She felt danger. Then Sara caught sight of her own shadow. *The light's gonna disappear*, she thought, *and the smoke's gonna come.*

"Ceapé, please answer me." Hot tears stung her eyes. Suddenly, Sara heard a soft sound coming from a clump of dandelions. She froze and, laboring to listen, she heard another slight rustle.

"Ceapé, is that you?" The thick growth hurt her bare feet as she ran through the grass towards the sound. Looking down, she saw a frightful sight. Ceapé lay shaking in a small hole, her head tucked under her wing. As she panted, her small white body lifted and fell in a fast rhythm.

"Ceapé."

"Don't—don't come near me, child . . . Tesps . . . run for your life!" As she spoke, Ceapé lifted her head. Sara bit her lip hard. She saw enormous licelike creatures covering Ceapé's eyes. Some were even on her body.

Those things are eating on her, thought Sara. And she let out a scream. "Ceapé!!" Some Tesps rose from Ceapé's body and flew towards her. Pulling herself into a tight ball, Sara clamped her arms over her face. She felt Tesps drumming her body with their wide, white wings as they shrieked and swarmed over her.

Sara quivered and struggled to keep from fainting from their awful smell.

I'm gonna die, thought Sara.

Again her mind filled with words from Mrs. Mole's book.

"The wise listen to advice."[6]

That's it! Sing—I've got power if I sing . . .

Somehow, with all the strength left in her, Sara drew in

a breath and began to sing a song her mother used to sing to her at night.

"I see the moon, the moon sees me . . ." Her voice only made a whispery sound, but she felt the creatures closest to her mouth back off.

". . . through the leaves of the old green tree."

Encouraged now, she sang louder.

"God bless the moon, and God bless me . . ."

They drew back and circled, buzzing about her head. Sara stood up, lifted her arms into the air, and sang at the top of her lungs.

"And God bless the ones I love!"

Running to Ceapé, she stood over her and sang her song again and again in a clear, strong voice until every Tesp vanished. Then she fell on the bird's neck and sobbed.

It felt to Sara that she could cry forever, but when crying is over, it's over. She rubbed her eyes with the tail of her shirt and blew her nose on a soft piece of leaf. Then she lay exhausted under her friend's wing.

The dark smoke rolled over the Meadow, but Sara and Ceapé were safe. At least for the moment.

"Wherever did THOSE awful things come from?" asked Sara.

"They're blind pests that live under the feathers of the Snedoms—waiting for a victim. After the Snedoms—" Ceapé's voice dropped to a whisper, "—got through with me, I knew the Tesps would come. I was just too weak to sing them away." Ceapé quivered at the horror of it all.

"If they're blind, how can they find you?" asked Sara.

"They smell their way to finish off . . ." She began to cry.

"Well—you're safe with me now, and I'm gonna get you to my treehouse. Do you think you can move?" Sara sat up now and forced herself to look closely at Ceapé.

Sara's eyes filled with tears when she saw her gentle friend's face streaked with blood, her eyelids swollen and sealed. "Oh, I *hate* that terrible Krad!! Death to him, terrible death!"

The anger that surged through Sara filled her with energy. "I gotta get you out of here." Sara began to pace under the dandelions. "The Snedoms are probably perched and watching us through the smoke. Let me think. Ah—"

Sara broke off a piece of honeysuckle vine, stripped off its leaves, and tied it loosely around Ceapé's neck. Sliding her arms underneath her soft, weak body, Sara boosted Ceapé to her feet. "Try to move . . . good. Now I'll guide you," she whispered hoarsely. "Trust me."

The thick swirling smoke frightened Sara. The music of the river was silent. Not a blade of grass sang a note. Then Krad's shrill scream split the air and shook the ground. Shivering, Sara tugged on Ceapé's honeysuckle vine.

"Hurry," urged Sara. "I know it's hard, but try, dear one. Try."

"We'll have to go through Gered's territory—then west to the olive tree. We have no time to go around," Ceapé said faintly.

Sara did not want to run into grumpy old Gered, but looking at her weak friend, she knew they must risk the shortest route. Ceapé fell often as she tried to walk.

"Do you want to rest?" asked Sara stroking her neck feathers.

"No, we mustn't stop," answered the bird. And coughing from the smoke, she slipped her head under her wing. Sara stood beside her.

"Here's where Gered's path starts. Stay close to me." And then they entered Gered's territory, both of them afraid and silent.

The path seemed invisible in the dark, and Sara found her way by keeping her bare feet on the smooth hard trail. She felt as blind as Ceapé. They covered quite a distance. Sara had begun to think that they had escaped Gered's notice when . . .

"Stop! I command you to stop in the name of the law!" Gered stood upright on the path with her black eyes snapping in the smoke. Her fierce quills flared.

"So, Miss Nosy, you're back to steal my food, is ya? I warned ya. You can't say I didn't warn ya," Gered roared.

"Don't be so dumb. Can't you see I'm just taking Ceapé through here to my house?" Sara's voice was loud and strong, but her body shook.

"Dumb is I, Miss? Well, I ain't as dumb as you thinks! I know a sneak when I sees one. You's slippin' in my territory to steal my food!"

"Let me explain—" said Sara.

"Shut up! I sees what you're about. Don't say I didn't warn ya."

In the shadows Sara saw Gered turning. Pulling hard on the vine tied to Ceapé, Sara yelled, "Hop, Ceapé, fast!"

Gered swung her outspread tail.

"Ohhh—ohhh," Sara cried, as she felt the needle-sharp barb stab the back of her leg.

"Don't blame me," Gered shouted after her. "Ya made your choice to come in my territory. I warned ya that this place is off limits. So don't blame me!" Gered swaggered down the path, gloating in her victory.

"Oh, it hurts, it hurts!" cried Sara, rolling on the ground, holding her ankle.

"Here, child. Let me help you." Ceapé panted hard from the effort to get away from Gered. "If you can force yourself to be still, I can pull the quill out with my beak. Now be brave, love. Help me get a hold on the thing."

Sara's whole leg trembled with pain. Holding her thigh with both hands, she pushed her leg rigid against the ground. "Oh—it hurts, it hurts."

Ceapé found the quill, clamped her beak around it, and jerking it hard, pulled it out. Ceapé toppled over, and Sara rolled on her side hugging her leg to her chest.

"Oh, I've never had anything hurt me so," Sara sobbed from pain and anger.

"The quills of Gered are dangerous, very dangerous." Ceapé could barely speak now. It had taken the last bit of her strength to help Sara.

"I'll never come this way again. Never!" Sara got on her knees and tried to stand. She let out a low moan. Gritting her teeth, she stood up and tried to hobble about. Tears ran down her cheeks, but she made no sound except an occasional sniff from her dripping nose. "Come, dear Ceapé. I'm gonna find us a hiding place."

Sara, limping badly, and Ceapé, barely creeping, finally made the last few feet to a group of rocks. "Duck down here. I'll cover us up in the leaves." Then Sara whispered hoarsely, "I will save you, Ceapé. I will!"

11

HELP COMES!

CEAPÉ'S TINY LEGS collapsed under her weight, and she sighed. She doubted that the child could hide them from the roving eyes of Krad. He could see right through the soupy dark smoke. But too weak to explain, Ceapé lay still. Besides, they had done their best, and there was no need to terrify the child.

With small strong hands Sara dragged five large sycamore leaves one by one to cover the bird. She had just buried herself deep in the hiding place beside her friend when she heard a faint hum. Sara froze. Her stomach flipped over.

"Don't move," she whispered to Ceapé. Sara could feel the presence of someone in the smoke just beyond them. She held her breath.

"I say, it's me, Dink! I've been searching all over for you chaps. I've come to help. You're almost to the leaf house."

Sara reached out, grabbed Dink, and held onto his comforting soft fur. "Oh, we've had such an awful time . . ." Sara began to cough.

"Shhh, my pet, don't talk in this smoke. First I need to get you home. Can you walk if you hold on to me?"

Dink scooped his front paws under Ceapé's feathered body and hugged her to his chest. Sara leaned heavily against him as he carried Ceapé. She could hear Snedoms hissing above them, and she pushed herself to limp faster.

With her eyes burning and watering, Sara stumbled through the smoke. Finally, Dink nudged her. They had made it home to the olive tree.

Dink slipped through the leaf door. "Under the boulder. Follow me." He scurried beneath the flat rock to the cavern below. "Ah, now we're safe." Gently he laid Ceapé on some soft gray moss. "She's in pretty bad shape. I need some light in here." Immediately, Dink began to glow.

Sara could see Ceapé's head had fallen to one side. "Oh, Dink, is she—dead?"

"No." Dink had his ear against her chest. "I can feel her breathing. Be quick—get some water from the mushroom cap upstairs. And do be careful."

Sara left the circle of Dink's glow and went to the main floor. Fumbling in the dark, she finally found some clean moss. Soaking it in the water, she carried it down to Ceapé. Then she gently washed the bird's face and cleansed her wounded, bloody eyes.

"Let me see that leg of yours, pet. Oh, I say! Nasty wound there. Gered can be an evil bugger, she can." Dink bathed Sara's ankle. She couldn't tell if it was Dink's comforting touch or the magic of the water that stopped the pain, but at once she felt better. She relaxed her aching head and bones against Dink. Her eyes closed, and her lashes rested on her dirty cheeks.

The next thing Sara knew, she was yawning and stretching in a bed of gray fur. She wiggled her toes and sat up.

"Well, pet, you slept soundly curled up in my tail."

The memory of all that had happened flooded into Sara's mind. "Ceapé?"

"I'm ever so much better." Ceapé's soft cooing flooded the room with music. "Thanks to you."

Sara put her weight on her injured leg to test it. "Good, it doesn't hurt at all." She stood up and skipped in circles. "This is great! I'm good as new! How'd I heal so fast?"

Dink smiled. "The water in the mushroom is from the River Elif. It flows from Lamper's Banquet Hall and has wonderful healing powers."

Sara stopped skipping and turned to look at Ceapé. The swelling had vanished, but her eyes remained tightly closed. "Does the water, I mean, could it heal . . . ?"

"One never knows the way of the river, my pet." Dink gazed at Ceapé and then looked away, sadly shaking his head. "Today we'll take her to Mrs. Mole's and see if anything can be done. She's fortunate to have her life."

"Indeed I am fortunate," Ceapé said. "And I thank you both for your tender care."

Sara ran to her side and draped her arms about the bird's neck. "I'm the one who needs to thank you—both." Then she hid her face in Ceapé's feathers.

"Before we travel, I must see to some proper food for you," said Dink.

The very mention of food made Sara's mouth water. It seemed like weeks since she had sipped honey tea at Mrs. Mole's. So after helping Dink move Ceapé into the soft fur-lined bed in the upper story of the leaf house, Sara followed Dink in search of food.

The Meadow, awash with light, warmed her body and her spirits. And every tree and flower, playing a secret instru-ment, lifted its song. Dink's lovely hum filled the air as he dashed about, and Sara lifted her feet and began a joyful dance.

How weird, she thought as she twirled about, *I almost got killed, am starving to death, can't find my way home, but because of light and music I'm dancing. This IS a strange place.* Bowing to a resting butterfly, she spied something familiar lying in a tangle of morning glory vines.

"Oh, look. It's Andrew's cap!" Picking it up, she tried it on. The cap covered her ears, slipped over her eyes, and rested on her nose. "Won't he love this? Dink, look what I found!"

The tattered baseball cap stirred up worry in Sara about her cousin. She had been gone a long time. And after all, being older, she was really responsible for him.

"Oh, I say, chappie," laughed Dink looking up from his search among the flowers. "You look quite fine under the cap."

"Good light to you both." Behind them, hopping on soft paws, came Teleng, Reca, and their family. Brown baby bun-nies tumbled and hopped everywhere.

"I knew you needed this, you poor child." Reca held out

a pine needle basket covered with a blue-checkered tea towel. "Blackberry muffins and honeysuckle nectar. Come, come now and eat. You need your strength."

She led the way into the olive tree house and put her basket on the gray rock table. She sat Sara on a stool, tucked the napkin under her chin, and served up the food on a pink flower petal, talking all the while.

"Your adventure would have been a horror for a Named One, but for such a child . . . I just don't know how you were so brave. And you, Ceapé, we must take you to Mrs. Mole right away. Perhaps she'll know if there's anything that can be done by reading from one of her ancient books." Reca plumped up Ceapé's fur bed and stroked her head. Then she turned back to Sara.

"Go ahead now, eat—eat, child."

Sara had never tasted anything so wonderful in her life. She stuffed her cheeks with sweet muffin and sipped the rich nectar. Then her eyes swept over Ceapé. "Oh, dear one, do you want some muffins? They're delicious."

"No, I must only eat at Lamper's table. I'll wait until that time," answered Ceapé.

"Oh, dear. Please pardon me for saying this, but you may not—I mean, what if you can't—" said Sara stumbling over her words.

"You think because I am blind, I won't have a way to the Banquet? Lamper will not forget me. I am his Named One—his Ceapé," the bird said softly.

"But who will take you? You're so weak. How will you travel? I'll ask Dink," said Sara.

"My child, don't worry yourself. I will be cared for."

"But I DO worry. We gotta make definite plans. It's good sense. And that's a fact." Sara licked her lips as she drank down the last bit of nectar. "I use my brain and figure things out."

Teleng, who had come in and overheard the conversation, patted Sara with his soft, brown paw. "But you see, we don't live on good sense alone here in the Meadow. Using good sense means you only make sense out of what you see. What you don't see would be left out. And what you don't see, my little one, is most of what is real."

Sara decided to change this confusing talk. "How did you know where we were?"

"Remember I told you the Named Ones know when certain things happen in the Meadow? We knew you were searching for Ceapé and making a map. And we knew you got mixed up with Gered," said Reca.

"Why didn't anyone come sooner?"

"Each of us has special tasks. Rescuing Ceapé belonged to you. Our job was to keep the faith for you," said Reca.

Sara drew her forehead into a frown. "What do you mean, 'keep the faith'?"

Reca looked at Teleng. He shook his furry head. "That's not for us to tell you," said Teleng.

"Well, I want to know!" Sara stomped her bare foot and jammed her hands in the pockets of her jeans. "There are too many secret facts around here. It's not fair!"

"It's not up to us to disclose secrets, my child," said Teleng, twitching his nose. "That's Lamper's business."

"Then help me draw my map, and I'll go to Lamper myself. I don't really care about his dumb old secrets. I just want to get Andrew and go home. All of you know the way to Lamper's. Why won't you help me?"

Sara had had enough of this double talk. In fact she had had enough of this adventure and just wanted to eat Rice Krispies and strawberries in her Aunt Janet's kitchen.

"We can join you once you're on the way, but I'm afraid we can't take you," said Reca stroking Sara's hair.

Sara jerked away. "Well, I think that's mean. Just plain mean!"

"It's not a matter of being mean, pet. You have been called into training, have you not?" asked Dink.

"Ah . . . ahh, I guess so."

Dink stood high on his back feet with his tail in a bushy question mark. "And you decided you didn't want to enter in?"

Sara pulled her chin to her chest for a moment. Then her green eyes snapped up at Dink.

"Well, Mrs. Mole wouldn't give me enough facts. But I said I would, since Andrew was so hot-headed and volunteered for training. Then she wouldn't even let me." Sara slapped her hand hard on the table. "So, you see, it isn't MY fault."

"You know that's not why, my child," said Reca. "You must let your 'yes' be yes and your 'no' be no."

"If you won't help, I'll make the map myself," pouted Sara. Feeling for the marking rock in her pocket, she sat on the floor in the corner and unrolled her piece of bark. *I'll just figure everything out with my own mind and take care of myself*, she thought.

A white circle and the words *Gered's Territory* were her last marks. Now she wrote "off limits" in bold letters across this space. Then she added "Leaf House."

While drawing, she could hear Dink and Teleng talking and Ceapé's soft cooing behind her. Peeking at Ceapé, Sara's heart turned over. *Ceapé just can't stay—stay blind*, thought Sara. *Mrs. Mole has to do something . . . Mrs. Mole and all her secrets*.

"Well, I think we're ready now," said Reca, who swept the last of the blackberry muffin crumbs from the table with her furry paws. "Please collect the bunnies, Teleng. I think we ALL should go with the child and Ceapé to Mrs. Mole's."

SARA'S CHALLENGE

A S THE GROUP set off down the path, they were a strange parade. Teleng, with his long brown ears erect, led the way, carrying Ceapé in his front paws. Hurrying along holding up his gray tail like a flag, Dink tried to help Reca keep up with the eight brown frolicking bunnies. With Andrew's cap falling over her eyes, Sara walked behind everyone making marks on her map.

Sara glanced down at her ankle as she walked. *So strange,* she thought, *there's not a sign of a jab from that awful quill. Not even a scar.*

"Someone tell me about that mean old Gered," yelled Sara from the back of the group.

Dink, letting the others pass, dropped back beside her. "Why don't you ride a bit," he said lowering his tail, "and I'll tell you about Gered." Sticking her map in her back pocket, Sara climbed up on Dink's soft back and put her arms about his neck. She could hear his comforting, soft hum from deep inside him. Even when he talked, the hum sang beneath his words.

"You want to know about Gered. Well, Gered started out

like the rest of us in the Meadow. She lived where she lives now. She knew about Lamper and Krad. She'd heard all the stories about the rebellious Laho and how Lamper renamed him Krad and sent him away from the light. Gered enjoyed the light and stayed out of the smoky dark."

"Sounds like the other Meadow animals," said Sara.

"Well, pet, she was—until she was called into training. Gered wasn't a bit interested. She said, 'Maybe later,' so I've been told. She had too much to do for herself. Anyway, she wanted to be independent and make a go of it on her own."

"What's wrong with being independent?" asked Sara.

"You can't be totally independent and be a creature of the light. We give our lives and love to each other," said Dink. "But being a creature of light didn't interest her. A lot of Named Ones tried to talk sense into her. But she's stubborn, and she shut her mind. Then Krad sent a few Snedoms over to invite Gered to join him. Those lying Snedoms told her she'd made a wise decision. They wanted to make her a witch of the dark smoke."

Sara trembled thinking of her encounter with Gered. "Well, what did she decide? Is she really a witch? She sure acts like one!"

"Well, pet, Gered just snorted at the Snedoms. Said she would never take sides, and then she slapped her tail and spread her threatening quills. Since then the Snedoms don't bother with Gered." Dink shook his head.

"Why not?" asked Sara. "I thought Krad and his Snedoms were after everyone."

"Not if they already belong to him. You see, if you don't choose the light, you're siding with the dark—and Krad."

"That's not fair! Not fair at all! Who made up that rule?" Sara held Andrew's cap on her head as Dink picked up speed.

"Fair? It's not a matter of being fair. It's just the way things are, and that, my pet, *is* a fact of the Meadow."

"She's just minding her own business," said Sara. "That's what she said." Sara couldn't believe she was defending awful Gered. But it was a matter of principle.

"Minding your own business delights Krad. It keeps your mind off of what he's doing. Besides if one is undecided about the light, he has automatically decided for Krad— whether he knows it or not," said Dink flicking his small pointed ears. "He's what we call an Undecided Decided. Ah, there's Mrs. Mole's up ahead."

That ended Sara's questions for the time being. The little group passed down the mushroom-lined path to the entrance, following Teleng. Dink stopped. Sara hugged his gray neck and slid off his back.

Reca lined up her bunnies. "Each of you must hop behind me in your finest behavior. It's a great honor to visit Mrs. Mole." Reca bent near them, her ears dipping forward, her face serious. "Listen and learn!"

"I can't wait to see Andrew," said Sara, surprised that she was eager to be with her troublesome cousin. "He'll be glad I found his cap."

The light from Ceapé, Teleng, Reca, and Dink made the tunnel as bright as the Meadow. Sara was amazed by the good behavior of the tumbling, scampish bunnies, who, with solemn little faces, followed their parents.

"Listen!" Dink sat up on his haunches and fluffed his tail. Mrs. Mole's song in her strong clear voice floated to them. Then Reca, Teleng, and Dink lifted their own songs in response.

As Sara listened, she became aware that, even though everyone had his own song, the songs worked together in perfect harmony. She wished she had more to sing than "I See the Moon."

Mrs. Mole, radiant in glowing brown velvet fur, stood up from her work at the spinning wheel and stretched out her forepaws. "I've been waiting for you. I have the honey tea steaming hot."

Mrs. Mole's black eyes blazed, and her short, stiff whiskers jerked up and down when she saw Ceapé lying limply in Teleng's arms. She placed her powerful claws over Ceapé's eyes. "I hate what has happened to you. You'll stay here with me." Then she turned to Sara. "I am glad you heard the call of your heart and went after our Ceapé. You have a brave spirit, my child."

"Oh, can't you do something, Mrs. Mole. I mean, you seem to know everything. And somewhere in all these mysterious books it must tell you how to cure bl—blindness." Now Sara felt foolish wearing Andrew's cap. Pulling it off, she tucked it under her arm. Then she glanced around the circular room. *Where is he?* she wondered.

Mrs. Mole shuffled to the middle of the room. Her pear-shaped body glowed brighter than all the other creatures.

The tiny bunnies hid their eyes from the light and lowered their ears to the floor. She stood for awhile without moving a whisker, and then broke her silence with a deep sigh. "I am afraid this is entirely out of my hands."

"But what about your magic books?" Sara's mouth began to run ahead of her brain. "I mean, I found one that talked to me when I opened it, and it even—I mean—ah—"

"You opened a book without permission," said Mrs. Mole. Sara blushed. "Did that book tell you how to cure blindness?" asked Mrs. Mole.

"No," said Sara, hanging her head.

"I was born blind, my child," said Mrs. Mole in a gentler voice. "Living blind was normal for all moles. And Lamper's light and Krad's dark were the same to me. I lived underground. But deep within I had a longing . . ."

Eyes locked on the glowing form, Sara waited for the story when suddenly Andrew fell into the room.

"'Scuse me, but Godo nearly caused an earthquake croakin' in the burrow. He's been out in the Meadow and—"

"And out of my way." Godo let out a lusty croak causing the bunnies to run under their parents. "I'll do my own reportin'. Good, good, you're all here. I won't have to send my thoughts out—so hard for me, ya know. I fall asleep and start dreamin'. Dreamin' about warm rocks to lie on and deep mud to—"

"Godo!" said Teleng. "Tell us what's going on."

"Yes!" Reca stomped her large hind foot. "You nearly scared the little ones to death with your croaking."

Godo, dropping mud from his lumpy body, took two

stretched hops into the middle of his friends. Dink went behind him, sweeping up the mess with his bushy tail.

"Ya know, exercising isn't my pleasure. In fact, ya know, I think I was born to take it slow and easy."

"Please, Godo," said Teleng wiggling his ears impatiently. "Get to the point."

"O.K., O.K., ya know it's hard for me to stay on track. Let me just croak it out. We're in DANGER!"

Mrs. Mole put her claws on Godo's head. "It's important that you settle yourself and concentrate."

"By golly, you're right. Yes, ya are. Everythin' hinges on my thinkin' . . . oh my," Godo croaked again. "I think I've forgotten." He blinked his yellow eyes hard.

Mrs. Mole closed her eyes. Sara watched Teleng, Reca, and Dink do the same. Their light grew more intense. Sara looked at Andrew. He too had his eyes closed. She noticed how shiny his face seemed under his golden blond hair. No one made a sound except Godo, who snored for a moment and then joined the quiet.

Suddenly his eyes blinked wide open. "Krad's making a filthy plan—for all-out war," he croaked. "Thanks gang for helping me think."

"Good work," said Reca rubbing Godo's back with her furry paw. "Got all the way down near Krad's cave, did you?"

"So that horrible Krad thinks he can take us! Well," said Sara jumping to her feet, "I say NEVER!"

Sara's feet began to tingle. She felt like she did when she rode on the big roller coaster at the state fair—excited and frightened at the same time. Turning to Mrs. Mole, she took in a deep breath.

"If you'll still have me, I am ready to go into training!"

"Sara!" Andrew reached out to touch her, but Mrs. Mole put up her broad forepaw. He dropped back.

"What you are doing has a great cost. The training, as difficult as it is, will be nothing compared to the battle."

Sara looked into Mrs. Mole's searing eyes. She looked at Andrew. Training had changed him already. She could see that for herself. She turned to her friends and found their eyes riveted on her. Even Godo was wide awake and staring.

"Stacking up the facts, it seems like no choice IS a choice—a choice for Krad. I gotta make a choice for training. And somehow for Ceapé."

Mrs. Mole placed her claws about Sara's hands. Everyone began to sing and cheer. Teleng and Reca danced around the room, with bunnies somersaulting every which way. Andrew and Dink hugged Sara. Sara tingled with excitement. Everyone was lost in the joy of the moment until Mrs. Mole spoke.

"There's no time to lose. You'll have to excuse me. I must make a trip to Lamper for instructions. Take special care, children. Krad will get wind that you're both in training. He has his spies."

Mrs. Mole took off her yellow apron and slipped into a garment that neither Sara nor Andrew could quite see. Then she vanished down the burrow before Sara could even ask to go with her. After all, if she could get to Lamper, the adventure would be over.

The group settled in front of the fire, and a lively discussion broke out as they waited for Mrs. Mole's return.

"I think you're absolutely and completely wrong, Teleng," said Reca. "These children ARE the ones we've been waiting for."

"Now don't get so worked up," said Teleng, watching his wife's ears flop back and forth.

"Please, since we're the ones in training, I sure wish you'd tell us what's going on." Andrew felt more sure of himself with his corduroy baseball cap crammed over his blond hair.

Ignoring Andrew, Teleng continued his argument. "All we know is that someone made in Lamper's likeness will come to do battle for us. And you can't really say that these children are like Lamper." Teleng patted his wife.

"The training is to clean them up. Then you'll see," said Dink. "That chap has improved a great deal already," he said pointing at Andrew.

"Yeah, ya never can tell how a fellow looks until he's cleaned up," said Godo. "And she's still pretty dirty."

"You're a fine one to talk," said Sara, remembering her muddy climb over his lumpy body. "It's because of you I lost my shoes and got so filthy."

"That's not the only reason," said Andrew. "We came here dirty."

"Speak for yourself!" said Sara snapping her eyes at her cousin. "Boys are always dirty."

"Enough," a soft coo settled down the voices. "There are some secrets that even the Named Ones don't know. True, we've been given some hints about battle from the ancient books, but the facts are hidden. Certainly, there should be no quarreling among us."

"You're right, Ceapé. You're so right," said Dink. "Of all creatures, *we* should live in peace. How about some tea all around, chappies." And Dink poured the blue cups to the brim with the sweet honey tea and served everyone—even the baby bunnies.

SARA'S TRAINING

AFTER CEAPÉ'S WISE advice and a cup of hot tea, everyone waited peacefully for Mrs. Mole's return—everyone but Sara.

Reca gathered her bunnies by the cheery fire for a story, while Dink and Teleng played a board game that looked like checkers. Godo snored just outside the cavern. Much to Sara's surprise, she watched Andrew take a tiny brown leather book from the shelf, open it, and ask Ceapé a question.

"When did you get interested in studying? And how'd you get that book to open?" Sara's voice sounded sharp.

"The boy has permission to open and read the ancient books," said Ceapé.

"Yeah, it's really exciting. All about old battles with giants and seas that swallow up the enemy."

"I thought you didn't like to study." Sara crossed her arms and stared at Andrew. "So what's the deal?"

"I guess reading what the teacher makes you read is boring. But these are true adventures."

"You've got to be kidding. You really expect me to believe that?" Sara laughed. "What a dreamer!"

"The ancient books ARE true," said Ceapé. "Every word is true. Only one wisdom book can be opened by Meadow creatures. The rest remain sealed until they enter training."

Sara stopped giggling. She looked at Andrew poring over the words in another large leather book edged in gold. "O.K., smarty, then read to me."

"Read for yourself." The voice caught Sara in her meanness, and she looked up to see Mrs. Mole's glowing form in the doorway. "You have accepted training, so all the words are open to you now."

Blushing, Sara ducked her head. Then she chose a small, dark green book from the shelf and sat on the floor to read these strange words in the chapter titled "The Named Ones."

In the new name,
A secret's told.
A name is given.
A gift unfolds.

Just when she was about to ask what the riddle meant, Mrs. Mole beckoned to Sara and the others.

"First we must remain calm," said Mrs. Mole tying her long, yellow apron around her plump middle. "Lamper is with us. So Krad, in spite of his terrible roar, can never completely overtake us."

Crowding around her, the creatures nodded their heads up and down in agreement.

"Still, the situation is dangerous. Krad's planning all-out

war with his Snedoms and Tesps. He's even gathering in the Undecided Decided. The children's presence here has made him extremely nervous. And rightly so! The training of the children is the key to stopping this growing evil. Their training AND their willingness to battle for us." Mrs. Mole's fur stood out with electricity as her last words rang through the room.

Sara looked at the waiting faces of her friends. Their eyes searched her face. *Go into battle and fight that horrible Krad. There's no way I can count the cost. And can't they see, I'm a very little person? Certainly they can't expect ME to FIGHT for them.* Sara's mind spun a web of thoughts. *I know this isn't good sense . . . but something deep inside me says—* And she shouted, "Begin my training!"

Everyone cheered as Mrs. Mole without a word took Sara by the hand and led her away.

Mrs. Mole shuffled amazingly fast down the tunnel with Sara in tow. Sara ran to keep up. "Isn't Andrew gonna come with us?" She thought she'd feel more comfortable if they could train together.

"Impossible for the beginning. Everyone's training is different. We're all unique, you see." Mrs. Mole never missed a step as she spoke. "You need to focus on what you are doing. He would draw your mind away from your learning."

Turning sharply to the right, Mrs. Mole pushed a door open for Sara. They entered. The door swung shut. Mrs. Mole stood in the middle of the mirrored room, lighting up the ceiling, walls, and floor.

"Oh, my heavens," said Sara spinning around on her bare feet. Everywhere she looked, she saw her reflection.

Moving slowly to the wall, Sara placed her hands on the mirror. What looked like a forgotten street child looked back. Large eyes peered out of a filthy face, and black, greasy hair hung in strings around her cheeks. She was caked with dried mud, except where Dink had washed her ankle.

"I'm a mess! A real mess!" She tried wiping the palms of her hands on the back of her torn pants, but they seemed to get dirtier. She thought of how she had just been strutting around saying she'd go into training.

"How embarrassing. I—I never knew I was so dirty." Tears pooled in her eyes and splashed down her cheeks, taking the grime with them.

"Yes, see yourself clearly. This, my daughter, is where we all begin. And there is no beginning until we each open our eyes to the truth of ourselves." Mrs. Mole's voice was full of mystery.

"Now you are ready for your first secret. In training you are to call me by my Meadow name—Wimdos." The name sang through the air.

Sara stared at Wimdos whose closed eyes seemed to disappear into her furry face. And the intensity of her glow was blinding. Around her body appeared a blue ring of light. Wimdos spoke.

"What happens if you eat snow?

"Why can't you eat plants with fine hairs?

"How many pine needles does a pine tree have?

"How many hairs are on your head?

"How many scales cover a red fish?"

With an icy voice Wimdos fired her questions at Sara.

"Where were you when the stars were made?"

Sara fell to the ground. "I don't know. I don't know much of anything."

"Then you are ready to learn. Come to me. Kneel and answer the questions set before you."

With tears still running down her face and dripping off her chin, Sara knelt with shaky knees on the cold, mirrored floor. She was afraid to look up at Wimdos.

"Do you promise to go into training as Lamper's daughter of light?"

Sara's body began to tremble. "I promise."

From her deep apron pocket Wimdos drew out Ritips, and the razor-edged sword flared with light. When she laid the flat of the blade on Sara's head, the pungent scent of a fresh pine forest flooded over her and filled the room. "By Lamper's diamond sword of Truth, I call you into training."

As soon as the words were spoken, a bitter wind ripped at Sara, chilling her to the bone. She tried to cry for help, but her voice was frozen. Her tears froze her eyelashes shut, and frost collected on her lips. She fell like a block of ice to the floor. Then as quickly as she had been frozen, she began to thaw. Horrible burning prickles stung her feet and hands as her blood warmed and flowed. Finally, a warm, gentle swirling breeze bathed her body, and she fell into an exhausted sleep. A gentle voice broke into her dreams.

"Awake, daughter." Wimdos looked at her with black blazing eyes.

Sara jerked her sleepy mind to attention. "Wimdos . . . how long have I been asleep?" She pushed up from the mirrored floor and blinked her eyes at her reflection. Her sparkling green eyes seemed to have light all their own, and her shining black hair curled softly around her small, clean face. But seeing the black dirt streaking her neck and her filthy torn shirt showed her the need for more cleaning.

Sara lifted her face to Wimdos. "I'm afraid to ask what's next."

"You have been gifted with an excellent mind, my daughter. But you allowed your gift to make you proud. Now you have been cleansed of vanity. We should never mistake knowledge for wisdom!"

With her claws, Wimdos gently brushed Sara's curls back from her shining face. "Battle with yourself! Never allow the pride of knowledge to enter into you again.

"Now for your second secret. The Named Ones are trained to concentrate. Close your eyes, my daughter."

Learning to rule her thoughts came easier for Sara than for Andrew. She could keep her keen mind steady. Studying books and practicing piano had given her excellent training. But she did have trouble actually *seeing* Wimdos in her mind. She hadn't developed as keen an imagination as Andrew had—from his practice of daydreams and inventions.

"Whatever you do, you must never, never think into nothingness. Your goal is to see Lamper's light and hear his voice."

Wimdos's voice directed Sara's mental picture. "See my

body. Find my black eyes . . . now my whiskers. See the powerful light. Good. Hold the thought. Don't let go of that image . . . don't let go."

The outline of Wimdos's body began to stand out clearly in her mind. *I wonder how many whiskers she has . . . six on each side . . . I think rabbits have more. Whiskers are so stiff on Alex. I wonder how that cat's doin'*—

"Daughter, focus. Now concentrate on Lamper's light." The image of Wimdos began to fade, and she saw the light. After many stops and starts, Sara absorbed the idea. Once she did, the next step came easier.

"Concentrate on his voice, my child." Sara held her breath and listened.

The voice came. *You are deeply loved.* The words filled Sara and echoed through her body. With her eyes still shut, Sara lifted her face and smiled. She knew she had heard Lamper.

"Excellent. Knowing you are loved is the key to everything else. Remember to conquer your interrupting facts and questions when you try to focus. They will steal the communication between you and Lamper, especially communication about love."

Wimdos's eyes burned with light. "You must be able to hear Lamper speak to your mind in order to handle the sword, or else the sword can't help you."

Sara felt sick at her stomach. "The sword? Of course—the sword—to fight Krad." She mumbled her words to the wall and saw herself reflected hundreds of times saying, "to fight Krad." Beads of sweat stood on her forehead, and her flesh crawled.

"You will not be alone in this battle. Lamper will be with you."

She wasn't at all comforted. *So far Andrew has been no help at all. Well, almost no help*, Sara thought as she wiped her head on her shirt sleeve. *And I don't know how to use that huge sword.* For all the secret words and training, she felt unready and too small for a fight with evil.

RITIPS

A LOUD CRASH outside the door interrupted Wimdos's deep concentration. She pulled the heavy mirrored door open.

"I thought I heard you calling me," said Andrew rubbing his throbbing elbow. "But the door wouldn't open even by force."

"I wanted you to walk through the wall, straight through," said Wimdos.

"The wall?" Andrew looked wide-eyed. Sara stared at Wimdos.

"Yes, the wall. It's really just a bit of rearranging of a few atoms, and you go right through. Comes in handy if you're in a hurry for any reason. Watch." Wimdos walked towards the wall and without hesitation walked straight through it. When she left, so did her light.

Sara felt for Andrew's long arm in the dark and found it reaching for her.

"Brother, I must be seeing things," said Sara. "Nobody could really do that. It must be a trick." She was about to add that she needed to hear a few facts, and then thought better of it.

"Well, I just hope she comes back. I can't even find the door," said Andrew.

The glowing Wimdos reappeared, lighting up the dancing reflections of herself and the children. "Now do you believe me?"

"Wow, it must be some kind of physics," said Sara, "splitting atoms, changing matter, or—"

"What's important is that you can do it," Wimdos interrupted, "not that you can explain it. Many creatures miss the important things about living, thinking that knowing about things is the same as doing them. Now concentrate and follow me."

The hundreds of reflections of Sara, Andrew, and Wimdos was a dizzying experience and added to the problem of concentration for the cousins. But finally after many bumps from running into the wall, the children *did* pass through. It reminded them of the time they learned to ride a bike. First it seemed impossible, but once they got the feel of it, riding was as easy as pie.

"Andrew, pass through and return with Dink. I must introduce this little one to the sword." Sara visibly shuddered, but Wimdos ignored her, watching Andrew leave.

"Dink's skill as a swordsman is equal to mine," said Wimdos. "He'll teach you to fight."

Wimdos and Sara closed their eyes. Sara heard Lamper's mind speaking to her. *Look at your hands, my child.* Sara stopped rubbing her hands together and looked at her palms.

"Terribly dirty," she said shoving her hands deep into her pants pockets.

Show me. Lamper spoke sternly. Sara inched out her sweaty hands.

"Oh, no! Help! Please help me!" cried Sara as she saw slimy, smelly, black mud dripping from between her tiny fingers. She lifted up her hands, and the mud ran down her wrist onto her arms.

Sara stuck her hands straight out from her, but she couldn't get away from the sharp, skunklike smell. It burned her eyes and nose. She shook her hands hard. Stinking muck slung everywhere sticking to walls, floor, and ceiling. "Oh, I am so sorry!" Sara started bawling hard.

"Give your hands to me!" said Wimdos. And she clamped her claws around both of Sara's hands.

Screaming with pain, Sara tried to wiggle free, but Wimdos's claws gripped like a steel trap.

"My hands, my hands!" screamed Sara. "Let me go!" Within seconds her hands glowed with heat.

Sara slumped into a faint just as Wimdos let go. Then the rush of cool, healing water, such as she had felt from River Elif, bathed her small hands and aching head.

"Oh, how sorry I am to bring you pain." Wimdos gathered Sara into her furry lap and tenderly stroked her black hair. "But in training you are not simply cleaned. You are remade. Look at your hands."

Sara examined her palms, and then slowly turned her hands over. "Why, they're perfectly clean!" she said through her sniffs.

"And," said Wimdos, "they are full of light. Can you stand yet, my child?" She knew the strain of this part of the training. After all, Wimdos herself had gone through it.

Sara sat for a moment wiping her eyes and looking at her glowing hands. The light she saw coming from within her gave her new strength.

Wimdos pulled the diamond sword from her apron pocket, lifted it high over her head, and then cut the air swiftly with its intense light. "Its name is Ritips."

"Arise, shine, for your light has come."[9]

"Oh," said Sara. "It speaks!"

Wimdos split the air once again with the sword.

"Walk as children of light."[10] Ritips sounded as clear and powerful as a lightning strike.

Without a word Wimdos held out the hilt covered with pearls, rubies, and green emeralds to Sara.

"Ah, well, the sword seems way too long for me. And so sharp. I think someone else should handle it. Hey, look! My hands are really too small."

Ignoring Sara's excuses, Wimdos placed Ritips in her palm. The moment Sara's hands grabbed the hilt, strength rushed into her arms. Her body felt warm and tingly.

"I—I can!" Lifting the sword, she sliced the air. Ritips adjusted to Sara's size.

"If your eye is clear, your whole body will be full of light."[11]

The room seemed alive with the words and the strong smell of cedar and pine.

"My daughter, you will be taught to use it well."

As Sara deftly cut the air with the dazzling diamond light, she danced on her bare feet, watching the light display sparking in the mirrors.

"Death to Krad!" she yelled. "And death to his foul darkness!"

"On guard, pet. So glad to see you're ready!"

Sara turned to see Dink's black eyes flashing as he placed himself opposite Sara. He held a jet-black sword. Andrew stood behind him.

"How did you get in here?" asked Sara.

"Right through the wall," said Andrew. "Dink can do it, too."

"But of course, chappies. All the Named Ones can pass through, but we weren't allowed to let you observe that until now. Besides we are to limit the passing through to special situations—like escape from danger.

"Now, to serious training, pets. My sword looks like Krad's weapon." Dink hopped in dancelike steps, whipping the black sword with powerful precision.

Sara stood flat-footed watching the nimble Dink moving with purpose.

"Stand like so." Dink stood on his back feet, back straight, with one paw behind his back and his fluffy gray tail curled upright. He placed the point of his sword on the floor in front of him. Sara imitated Dink as best she could.

"Wait. You need these." Wimdos put a small brown leather face mask and vest on Sara.

"You and Andrew are much smaller than I am," said

Dink, "but I will show you how to take advantage of your size. There'll be no mercy for Krad!

"Now, on guard!" The squirrel raised his sword. Sara did the same, and the light and the dark crossed between them. As they fenced, Dink explained his secret thrust and foot-work.

"Watch your stance. Stay on your toes!" Dink bristled with excitement.

"Eyes on me. Chin up. Now move!" The squirrel and the girl worked hard for a long while. Then Sara let her shoulders slump.

"Oh, Dink, I'm worn out. Your turn." Sara handed the sword and mask to Andrew and dropped to the cool glass floor. "I gotta rest!"

Wimdos rubbed Sara's aching shoulders as they watched Andrew and Dink practice. The splendid Ritips left a trail of light as it flashed, and the sight filled Sara with awe. Sometimes as they worked, Ritips would speak. Sometimes it struck a blow with silent power.

Suddenly, the ominous black sword clashed hard, and Andrew lost his grip. Ritips crashed and went into a wild spin on the floor, throwing light like a merry-go-round.

"Maybe if I had my glasses, I could do better." Andrew jerked off the leather mask and hung his head. "I feel like such a klutz."

"Nonsense! You just need instruction and practice. You're both doing quite well for your first lessons. Back to work! Initial position. On guard!" said Dink.

After what seemed like hours to the children, Wimdos called the training to a halt.

"Time for you to go to the leaf house. Reca will bring you food. So eat and get some well-deserved rest." Wimdos hugged Andrew hard and pressed Sara deep into her fur full of light. "You need to travel while the Meadow is free of Krad's dreadful smoke. One last thing. Don't forget to practice concentrating. Lamper may have a message to send you."

"Yes, pets. Pay attention! Things are beginning to get hot around here," said Dink, and his whole body quivered with electricity as if he knew a threatening secret.

Danger at the Olive Tree

SARA LED ANDREW down the damp, dark burrow and out into the open. The Meadow was smiling with life and smelled like new-cut grass on a steamy summer's day. Yellow butterflies with large black spots flitted in playful pairs over a mix of pink, purple, and orange flower patches. Cocky grasshoppers hopped high in the wild green oats. Small, brown chickadees and fat, red-breasted robins chirped the latest gossip.

"Boy, there's a lot going on around here," said Andrew, pulling on the bill of his cap. He squinted, trying to make out something down the path. "Hey, what's that?"

"I don't know. Looks like some kind of a rock—a moving rock." Sara put her finger to her lips. "Shhh!"

As they stood like statues, a large, dark brown, round object inched into some thick, stickery blackberry vines.

"Who are you?" Sara yelled in her biggest voice. No one answered, and she was relieved.

"Whoever's there is not very friendly," said Andrew watching as the creature completely disappeared in the overgrowth.

"Well, since the light is with us, I don't think we're in any danger. Come on. Let's sing as we go by—just in case."

"I see the moon, the moon sees me . . ." Andrew joined in. "Through the leaves of the old oak tree . . ."

As the children walked by the tangle of vines, there were no signs of life, and they were glad. Even though they were in training to be Named Ones, neither felt sure of winning a fight with one of Krad's spies—yet.

Now as they continued to the olive tree, Sara had a chance for the first time to share her adventures with her cousin. She told him about the search for Ceapé, the run-in with Gered, and the attack by the terrible Tesps.

"And if Dink hadn't come to our rescue, something more horrible than blindness would have happened to Ceapé and to me—*death!*" She whispered the word.

"Wonder why Dink or the rabbits didn't help Ceapé? Everyone seemed to know she was in trouble. Mrs. Mole told me Ceapé had been blinded before you and Dink brought her home."

There are tasks assigned to each of you.

"What did you say?" asked Sara.

"I didn't say anything," said Andrew. Removing his cap, he slowly swung himself around and squinted hard, looking for another rocklike creature. Then he linked eyes with Sara. "Do you think we got a thought message from Lamper?"

"Let's try and concentrate," said Sara.

The two stood motionless with their eyes shut, waiting. Floating across their mind-pictures came interrupting thoughts. Sara fought questions, and Andrew fought day-dreams.

There are tasks assigned to each of us. The voice became clear in their minds.

"Does that mean finding Ceapé was my—*my job*? Is that what Reca meant?" asked Sara.

Good receiving, children!

"It IS Lamper. Wow! We did it, Sara! We did it! You know, I wish I could really meet Lamper." said Andrew.

Then Andrew pulled gently on Sara's ragged shirt. "Sounds to me like you were the only one supposed to go after Ceapé. I'm proud of you." Embarrassed, he ducked his head.

"If there's special stuff that only we can do, then I guess we really gotta pay attention," said Sara.

Andrew stepped behind Sara as the path narrowed and twisted around an enormous boulder. On the other side they saw their leaf house. And at the entrance sat a large straw basket covered with a cherry-red cloth.

"Look, we're home! And Reca must have left us some food." Sara dashed ahead and vanished into the house with Andrew at her heels. They explored their root house once again. The many rooms, the tiny fur-lined beds, and soft moss rugs were just as they had left them. And music from the tree filled every space.

"Could you ever imagine a more wonderful hideout. When we get back home, do you think anyone will ever believe we lived in a tree's roots?" Sara stopped talking and looked at Andrew. Sitting in the dirt, he fingered his prism and stared into space.

"Andrew! What's with you?"

There was a long silence. Finally Andrew said, "Do you think we'll ever *get* home?"

"Don't be a dope! 'Course we will. All we have to do is find Lamper."

"But what about our training? What about fighting Kr—Krad?" Andrew felt his heart bump in his chest. "Remember his horrible black cloak? His shrieking scream? Those gross-looking Snedoms? How could we expect to stand up to him? That's a real joke."

Sara was surprised that Andrew was so doubtful. She was the skeptical one. "Well, how would I know? But we are being given weapons and secret powers." Sara looked Andrew right in the eyes. "We can trust Mrs. Mole's training—don't you think?"

Andrew began to shake from the top of his head to the bottom of his feet. A picture of three black-winged Snedoms formed in his mind. They flew at his face, gripping him with their powerful scaly claws, ready to peck his eyes out with their razor-sharp beaks. "Oh, I can't, I can't—help—help!!"

"Snap out of it! Andrew!" Sara shook him by the shoulders. "Do you hear me?"

Andrew buried his face in his hands. His cap fell to the floor. Sara had broken apart his daydream, but he sat there still shaking.

"Wow! That was terrible. It felt so real." He wiped the

sweat off his face with his shirt tail and pulled his cap down over his ears.

"Maybe our greatest enemy is not Krad, but fear," said Sara. "Come on. Let's forget about this for awhile and go look for something to eat in that basket."

When Sara slipped out of the house, she noticed the Meadow had begun to smell smoky. The light was beginning to close up. Hurriedly she dragged the heavy basket back in. The smell of cinnamon and sugar icing came in waves as she lifted the red napkin off the fat rolls.

"Look at these," she said, trying to coax Andrew. "And here's lots of butter and something to drink." Andrew knelt down beside her. His stomach growled with hunger.

"This looks great!" The sight of food seemed to brush away the black dream. "Hey, these are still warm," he said lifting a roll to his mouth. He was a second away from biting down when a strong voice came to his mind.

Do not eat! He stopped and looked at Sara as she buttered her roll. Now his cinnamon roll smelled better than ever. The sugar icing dripped onto his fingers. The voice, urgent and strong, came again. *Do not eat!*

Sara had her food halfway to her mouth when the same voice stopped her. Looking at Andrew, she saw him looking at her. But their hunger was so great and the smell so inviting that both children took a bite at the same time.

"Hmmm, how delicious." Sara stuffed the roll into her mouth and reached for another. Andrew ate as fast as he could, finishing his third before Sara ate her second.

"Hey, look. This is great. The basket's still full," he said, licking sweet white icing and warm butter off his fingers.

"Let's taste this," he said, pouring some spicy golden liquid from a small jar into two walnut cups.

Do not drink, my child! said the voice in his mind. But this time neither he nor Sara waited one second to put the cups to their lips.

"This is scrumptious," said Sara, after the first sip. And they both drank the sweet nectar as fast as they could. Then in place of the sweet taste, a piercing bitterness filled their mouths.

"Ick." Sara spewed the drink into the air. "Tastes horrible—like—like poison!!"

Andrew, coughing and sputtering, doubled over. "Oh, I need to get outside." He wobbled and bumped about the room. "I think I'm gonna be sick."

Sara grabbed her middle and groaned. "I AM sick. Oh, I want to go home." Both children fell out the leaf door and sprawled on the ground, rolling and crying, holding their stomachs.

"Help," Sara cried in a weak whisper. "Won't somebody help?"

The thick dark smoke, sticky and choking, rolled over the Meadow from the bowels of Krad's cave. In the blackness of his hole, Krad had called his forces together. Snedoms hissed and flopped as they roosted in the bare thorn trees above their master. Krad, his narrow head hidden under a drooping hood, paraded about in his long black cape. The Snedoms hovered over to listen.

Krad threw back his hood exposing his skull and let out a horrible scream.

> *Death to the children*
> *Who dare fight me!*
> *Tear out their eyes*
> *So they can't see!*

The Snedoms stretched their heavy black wings and hissed. Krad's ranting sounded across the Meadow like the voice of an evil giant.

> *Call out my forces*
> *Of evil and dark*
> *To grab those two children*
> *Who lay poisoned and marked!*

He let out a hideous howl, and the Snedoms lifted off their burdened perches and began to fly with purpose. The dark smoke swirled in clouds from the wind in their powerful wings as they headed straight for the olive tree. As they beat their wings against the smoky sky, they hissed and screamed out a death caw. Hundreds of them landed in the olive tree while others soared above like a sinister patrol.

Andrew heard the ominous sound of the Snedoms and felt the evil pressing down, but he couldn't lift his head. Sara, dead silent, lay rolled up in a ball a few inches from him.

Oh, Lamper, forgive me. I didn't listen to you, thought Andrew. The last thing he remembered was the putrid smell of rotten eggs and that horrible, constant hissing.

Krad's howl echoed through the smoky haze, urging his troops towards their kill.

> *Death to the light.*
> *Strike with Krad's might.*
> *Darkness is right.*
> *Death to the light!*

"Down," hissed Selfa, the leader. And thirteen nasty Snedoms dropped towards the children with their claws spread and ready. The Tesps rode on the Snedoms' bodies. They would finish feasting on the leftovers.

"Now!" screamed Selfa as he stretched one powerful clawed foot out to grab Sara and hold her in his clutches. But a tremendous jerk moved Sara just in time. The claw smashed into the dirt. Sara was jerked again. This time she disappeared into the leaf house.

Selfa screamed in rage. Two other Snedoms moved in to grab Andrew. Something thin, red, and sticky whipped around his waist, yanked him hard, and bumped him over the rough ground into the tree root.

"Kill!" yelled Selfa.

Now at their leader's command, a hundred Snedoms flopped down from their roost in the tree, snapping off branches as they came. Flopping and hissing, they beat their giant wings at the opening and ripped off the tree bark with their beaks. After leaving their putrid smell around the base of the tree, they heard a violent croaking cough and then silence.

Suddenly, a streak of light cut through the smoke. Light was coming from the mountain.

"Retreat!! Retreat!!" shrieked Selfa, and the Snedoms lifted up from the ground and the trees, flapping hard to return to the cave away from the piercing light. Now they had to face the terrible rage of Krad. But to creatures of the dark, that would be less painful than seeing themselves in the light.

16

THE RIVER ELIF

IN THE MEANTIME, Mrs. Mole had sensed the children's trouble and sent the rabbits to the rescue. Teleng and Reca hopped as fast as they could through the Meadow—until they saw the olive tree. They stopped stone-still, frozen at the sight.

Great branches lay broken on the ground among the leaves. Strips of bark, torn from the trunk, hung over bushes, and black feathers blanketed everything. Andrew's baseball cap dangled from a twig by the treehouse door.

"Oh, no!" Teleng rubbed the red scar on his forehead. "I hope we're not too late!" He whistled. "The smell's awful."

They moved through the piles of feathers and bark to the tree base and, holding their noses, squeezed inside.

"Let's light up. I can't see a thing," said Reca as she began to glow. She shook her ears at Teleng after hopping from room to room. "I can't find them."

"I'll try below," said Teleng. He scrambled under the boulder. "Here! Here they are. Help me. Will you look at this! Godo's down here."

The rabbits lifted the limp bodies of Sara and Andrew

out into the light. Then by pushing and shoving, they moved Godo's large, lumpy body through the opening and into the Meadow.

"Rub their faces," said Reca as she took Sara's small face in her soft, brown fur paws. Teleng did the same for Andrew, gently rubbing his forehead and cheeks. The children moaned.

"Let's work on Godo." Both the rabbits rubbed on Godo's wide face and round brown and green spotted back. Finally, he let out a sputtering croak.

"Oh, my good buddies. So glad to see ya." He slowly blinked his eyes. "That stinkin' bunch nearly did these kids in. And knocked me for a loop, too. Their smell has quite a kick."

"What happened around here?" asked Reca, rubbing Godo's front leg.

"Almost lost the kids, I tell ya." Godo croaked weakly. "Still might. They got into some poison. I got wind of the plan while I did a little sleepin'. One of the old Senparps was sent to stock the kids' place with poisoned grub—a care package from Krad. Decided I'd better hop on down and hang around. Good thing I did, too."

"How did you ever save them?" asked Teleng.

"Had to jerk those little rascals in with my tongue," said Godo.

"Do you think you can hop?" asked Reca. "The children are barely breathing. Our only hope is to get them to the River Elif."

"Oh, sure. I'm a tough old toad."

Teleng and Reca lifted the children up in their front paws. They lay heavy and lifeless, like two rag dolls. The high grasses parted as the rabbits and Godo made their way to the river. The way seemed long with their burdens and, after hopping for quite a way, Reca called out to Teleng, "Please, slow down. I'm ready to collapse." Teleng stopped and gently laid Andrew down in a mass of blue lupin. Andrew groaned. Teleng patted him.

"We'll soon be there. Hold on, son. Hold on."

Reca and Godo caught up with Teleng.

"She's so heavy. My body's aching," said Reca as she carefully laid Sara in the flowers beside Andrew.

"Child, can you hear me?" Reca rubbed her cheeks. Sara's half-open eyes stared back.

"I think the kid's unconscious," said Godo. "Just a pinch of Krad's poison can be a killer."

Reca sighed. "I hope we can make it in time. I just had to stop and catch my breath."

"Me too. I'm done in. Couldn't hop another . . ." Godo began to snore.

"Dear Reca, we need courage and strength. Come, sing with me," said Teleng.

"Now?" asked Reca. "We can't sing now. We need to press on." A small tear made a wet trail on her furry cheek. "It's a fearful task! These children's very lives are in our paws!"

"Their very lives are in Lamper's hands. Come now, just to help me," said Teleng. "Sing." Reca twitched her whiskers and flicked her ears back and forth. Then she hopped to Teleng and leaned against him.

The moment they lifted their voices, the wild flowers, grasses, and trees, joining in with their own music, began to sway and dance. Godo's big eyes blinked open, and his banjo sound plunked out a cheerful tune.

The rabbits' last musical note blew off into the breeze, and Reca sighed.

"The strength has returned to my legs, and hope has returned to my heart." Then she reached down into the lupin and scooped up Sara. "Come on. To the River Elif!"

"To the River Elif!" shouted Teleng.

"To the River Elif!" croaked Godo.

Now as they picked up their pace, it seemed that every living thing encouraged them with music. Soon they heard the mighty rush of the river, and their ears were filled with the sound of its powerful symphony. Their bodies pulsed from the vibrations.

"We're almost there!" shouted Teleng, rounding a bend in the path.

"Hold it right there!" A creature half the size of Teleng guarded the trail. Its smooth head stuck out from its rough, dark brown shell. Tough, short legs ended in sharp clawed toes, spread wide to hold the animal's body up. Godo hopped up behind Teleng.

"It's you. You old bugger. That's him!" said Godo. "That's the leader of the Senparps that poisoned the kids!"

"For your information I am Neam." Neam spoke slowly and snapped his mouth around his words.

"Out of our way, Neam!" Teleng scratched his back foot sending dust flying in clouds. "You've done your damage."

"We Senparps must finish what we've started," said Neam. "If you hadn't interfered, it would be over. The children must die."

"Never!" said Reca.

Neam stretched his wrinkled neck straight out from his dark, thorny shell and lifted his head. "Senparps, attack!" The grass rustled from every side.

"Watch it! These rustlers have us surrounded." Godo puffed out his body as large as he could. Teleng and Reca pressed the children against their furry chests. Their rabbit bodies tingled in readiness. Their hearts thumped like drums.

"Go!" whispered Teleng. And all three of them leaped forward.

"Attack!" Neam thrust his head at Teleng and snapped. Catching the rabbit on the foot, Neam clamped down and cut through Teleng's fur into his flesh. Pain shot through Teleng. He screamed but hung onto Andrew with all his might.

Reca made it past Neam only to run into another crusty Senparp who grabbed her left two toes.

"Help! Help me!"

"Hold on, Reca," cried Teleng.

"Let me go, blast ya. Let me go!" Godo jerked his back leg, violently wagging the head of the Senparp who had gripped him. "You'll git yours, you scumbag." Suddenly the

Senparp, his mouth foaming, set Godo free. "Ha! Poison for poison!"

The other Senparps backed away from Godo. He turned to Reca and Teleng. "We're almost to the river. If you can git into the water, them Senparps will let go. Try to drag 'em."

The rabbits, clutching the children, and crying in pain hopped and dragged the Senparps. Godo leaped about Reca and Teleng with his bleeding leg, keeping the other Senparps at a distance.

"I can't . . . I can't make it." Tears poured down Reca's furry cheeks. She looked at the Senparp holding fast to her bloody foot. "Hideous! This is hideous!"

"Go, gal, go. Listen to this old toad. I'm keeping those other Senparp-devils away. They don't want another taste of MY poison. Now the river's ahead. Lift your chin. Look." Godo began his banjo sound.

Reca looked up. She could see the crystal clear water splashing and dancing against the bank as it cut though the Meadow with power. She drew in a great breath and began the painful hop-drag towards the river.

"Good goin'." Godo coached her all the way to the river's edge. "A few more feet. Now into the water with ya!"

Reca threw herself into the river—Sara, Senparp, and all. Godo leaped in beside her. Teleng, holding Andrew, fell in, too, with Neam holding fast to his foot.

"Now give them Senparps a hard shake. They'll come loose, they will!" Godo swam back and forth between the rabbits giving instructions. "Hang on to the kids. Shake again. Shake! Good goin'!"

Quite suddenly both Senparps let go and disappeared under the water.

"I'm free." Reca held Sara to her and let the tears fall. Teleng, still supporting Andrew, made his way to her side. Their feet dug into the shallow river bottom, and they leaned into each other to catch their breath, as Godo croaked and swam around them in circles.

"Now healing River Elif, by the power of Lamper, heal these children." Teleng lowered himself and Andrew into the water until the river splashed over their heads. Reca sank down with Sara in her arms. Only the rabbits' ears stuck out above the river's surface. They came up gasping for breath. Sara sputtered and lifted her head. Coughing and spraying water into the air, Andrew wrapped his arms around Teleng's neck. And with a hoarse whispery voice he spoke in Teleng's long ear.

"I'm wet!"

Teleng threw back his head and laughed. "So you are, my child. Wet and *alive!*" Then all of them clung together, washed by the music and the healing of the River Elif, laughing and crying in celebration.

17

THE SCAR

"HEY, LOOKA HERE." Godo, sitting on the river bank, soaking up the warmth of the light, stretched out his long, spotted leg. "I only gotta scar left. What a time . . ." Godo began to snore.

The rabbits carried the children from the river and stood them on the shore.

"Boy, are my legs shaky. I feel like a bowl of jello," said Andrew. He felt for his prism. The wet string was around his neck, and his fingers slid across the prism feeling its cold, cut glass edges.

"How can we thank you?" said Sara, rubbing her dark, wet hair with both hands "We—"

"Almost died," said Reca, trying to fluff up her soaked fur. "As far as we can tell, Krad sent that horrible Neam and his Senparps to trick you with poison cinnamon rolls. You see, they're some of the few evil ones that can venture out in the light. Living in their shells, they carry around their own black caves. The moment the light bothers them, they draw into themselves."

"Yes, you were to be poisoned by Senparps and finished

off by Snedoms. The Snedoms left their smell and their feathers. Looked like a wicked battlefield." Teleng rubbed the warm, prickly healed spot on his leg, remembering Neam's painful bite. "I'm just glad we were close to the river."

"What happened to you?" Andrew squatted down to take a closer look at Teleng's leg.

"All three of us had a run-in with a Senparp. Since Godo rescued you from the Snedoms, the Senparps had to stop us from getting you to the healing of the river. To complete their mission, you had to die. And they almost succeeded. They used a deadly poison," said Reca.

"But I got ole Neam." Godo lifted one eyelid. "Gave him some of my own poison for his bite."

"Oh, thank you. Thank you, all!" Sara cupped her hands and filled them with water. "And thank you, wonderful River Elif." Lifting the sweet cold water to her mouth, she drank. It was then that she noticed the dark purple scar on her right palm. "Andrew, let me see your hand." He, too, carried a scar.

"What's this from? Did the Senparps get me on the hand?"

The rabbits twitched their whiskers as they exchanged a knowing look.

"These are not the scars from a battle," said Reca thumping her foot.

"Were either of you forewarned not to eat or drink?" Teleng looked straight into Andrew's blue eyes.

Andrew looked away and kicked a small pebble with his wet tennis shoe. He wished he had his cap to pull over his

ears. "Well, ah, well—maybe. I mean, well . . . no, I really
don't think so."

"Did Lamper speak to your mind?" Teleng put his paw
on Andrew's shoulder.

"Well, ah . . ." Andrew felt hot. His face turned red.

"Sara, did you receive a warning?" Sara didn't answer
Teleng. A lump filled her throat, and her eyes burned with
tears.

"Children, only the truth will free you," said Teleng.

"Yea, 'fess up, kids. It's the only way," said Godo taking
another break from his nap.

There was a long silence. Everyone waited.

"Well, there's absolutely no factual basis to believe a
voice from someone else can speak to your mind," said Sara.

"And I couldn't be sure," said Andrew. "At the time the
hot sweet rolls seemed more real than the voice."

"But what do you say now?" asked Reca.

Andrew let himself remember the sound of his mother's
voice. He thought of Wimdos and the training.

Andrew dropped to his knees and covered his face to
fight back his tears. Shutting his eyes he knelt in concentration. *Forgive me, Lamper,* he thought.

Child of light, you are forgiven, Lamper answered.

"All of you have suffered 'cause I wouldn't listen. How
can you forgive me?" He felt he could never look at his
friends again.

"We forgive you, Andrew. Your scar is the scar from a
mistake. All of us carry these scars." Reca took Andrew's
hand in her paw. "Look now."

He saw that the bright purple streak had faded into a pink line.

"We carry the scars of our choices. But when we ask for forgiveness, they begin to fade. I have a few scars hidden in my fur. They remind me of my past."

"Well, you just have a good imagination, Andrew Stevens. I certainly didn't hear any voice!" Sara shoved her hands into the pockets of her damp jeans, lifted her chin, and jutted out her lower jaw. Reca put her paw on the top of Sara's head.

"That's too bad, child. That's too bad."

"Come on, folks. The Senparps are gone, but the light's soon to be shut in. This is no place for a good toad like me."

"Godo's right. Let's go to our hole," said Reca. "Teleng and I need to gather the bunnies from their play."

Reca's soft brown fur, washed in the river and dried by the light, caught Teleng's eye, and he stroked her ears with his paw. "You look beautiful, my dear."

Reca lowered her long eyelashes. "You're beautiful too, Mr. Rabbit."

"Home it is!" said Teleng. "I feel like a celebration." And he began to whistle a tune as he twirled his wife through the swaying wild flowers and grasses. The trees lifted their limbs and leaves, adding their music. And two small singing red birds encircled the rabbits as they danced.

Sitting and watching, Andrew felt the music fill him and break through his shyness. Suddenly, he felt nimble as a kitten. And before he could think about it, he found himself, arms lifted up, spinning and dancing.

"Come on, Sara. It's fun!" he said as he fell on the grass to catch his breath. But Sara sat folded up with her face buried in her knees.

The medley ended, and Teleng called Godo and the children to start the hop home.

"You folks head down the road. I'll be hoppin' to Mrs. Mole's. No offense, but I'm too bushed to put up with eight leapin' bunnies. I need to bury myself for a snooze." Godo leaped away into the tall brush. He gave a croak from a distance. "You kids stay out of trouble. Ya hear?"

Now Teleng picked up the pace along the river's edge. Andrew walked fast, but Sara, shoulders sagging and head hanging, shuffled behind. As she got farther and farther behind, the rabbits stopped.

"Child, you must try and keep up," said Reca. "We'll just go over the bridge, and in a few more hops we'll be home."

Just beyond the next rise, a log from an ancient oak tree lay from bank to bank across the crystal river. The log served as a bridge to the other side of the Meadow.

"Here we go. Hop behind me now." Reca went ahead. Andrew widened and rolled his eyes. Moving swiftly, the shining, rushing water splashed against the rocks in its path and wet the low bridge.

"It's—well, it's deep. And scary!" said Andrew.

The healing water now looked treacherous—full of danger. "I can't go across." Andrew froze at the end of the log. He could see himself being washed off the narrow bridge into the river. He saw his bobbing head. He heard his screams as the water washed over his head drowning him before anyone could save him.

"Come on. You can make it. Have faith and concentrate." Reca coaxed him from the other side. Andrew shut his eyes to quiet the imaginations and the "I can'ts" screaming in his mind.

Lamper, please speak to me, he thought.

He waited.

My son, walk in faith, Lamper spoke back.

Andrew fixed his eyes on Reca, sucked in a deep breath, and with rubbery legs took a step.

"Good going!" Teleng's voice rang out behind Andrew.

The water roared underneath him, and his heart thumped in his throat. He took another step and another. A piece of loose bark crunched beneath his shoe, and he slipped to the right. Barely catching his balance, he took one final leap and felt the Meadow under his feet.

"I made it! I made it!" yelled Andrew dancing a wild jig next to Reca.

"You're next, Child," said Reca.

Sara looked at the raging water splashing the bridge. "No! I'm not moving."

"The smoke will soon cover the Meadow. You can do it. Now concentrate," said Teleng.

Sara's eyes flashed. "I know danger when I see it. Andrew almost fell. Considering the wind factor, water depth, my size, and the distance, I have decided that I'm not moving." She put her hands on her hips and stuck out her lower lip.

"I'm ten times more clumsy than you are," shouted Andrew. "If I can make it, you sure can!"

"I've thought this out. I won't—" Before she could finish her speech, Teleng picked her up from behind and started hopping across.

"Ohh! I'm gonna die. Help!!" Sara kicked, screamed, and finally squirmed around enough to get a choke hold on Teleng's neck. Once on the other side, he pulled Sara from his neck, and she fell in a heap, crying and pounding her fist in the grass. "I wanna go home."

"Sara—" Andrew knelt down beside her.

"Get away from me, Mr. Goodie-two-shoes. You're a jerk and I hate you!"

"Hey, what did I do? Boy, can girls get mean!" Andrew stood up and backed away.

"She doesn't like herself right now," whispered Reca. "It really has nothing to do with you."

Then she took Sara by the hand. "Come along now. The hole is in sight."

Sara jerked away and jammed her balled up fists in her pockets. How she hated that red scar.

THE DRIPE DISEASE

A S THE GROUP journeyed to the rabbits' burrow, eight brown bunnies, bouncing and tumbling and full of questions, met them on the path.

"Well, Krad got quite a blow," said their father. "We escaped from that miserable Neam and his blasted Senparps. And I think this calls for a party!"

Teleng hopped about, lifting bunny after bunny into the air. Andrew rolled in the tall green grass, laughing and playing with his little friends, but Sara stood with her back to everybody.

I hate parties, she thought. *This is so dumb, I can't stand it.*

"Daughter, come help me." Reca's voice broke into Sara's grumbling. Without a word she followed Reca into the hole. "You can put the cups on the table there." Reca glanced at Sara's long face and drooping mouth. *So sad*, thought Reca. "I'm just going to stir up some poppyseed cake for you and the bunnies."

Sighing, Sara set the table, thumping the acorn cups hard on the wooden table. She clanked the pot of honey down and carelessly tossed the green napkins around at each place. Then she sat in a slump against the wall.

Reca worked silently in her kitchen, twitching her whiskers as she thought. Finally she decided to share her own story.

"When I was a young rabbit in training, I loved Mrs. Mole's ancient books. It seemed like the books called to me from the shelves, and I opened up the ancient pages to listen and listen. Somehow the secrets they shared made sense deep inside my heart."

Holding her head in her hands, Sara stared at the floor.

"Finally, after all my lessons from Wimdos, I got my invitation from Lamper. Then Wimdos told me that I was not to eat until I attended the Banquet."

Sara looked up at Reca stirring her pot.

Reca flicked her ears and continued. "But the strangest thing happened. I began to feel hungry. Very, very hungry. Floating in my daydreams, I saw and smelled bowls of steaming orange carrot stew and beautiful piles of wet green lettuce. All I could think of was food. The thought of fresh tomato pie made my mouth water, and the smell of sweet white radishes made my stomach growl." Reca wiped her paws on a blue tea towel and sat by Sara.

"I got so hungry that I began to hop around, scrounging for food. Then words came to me from the ancient books. '*Set your mind on things above, not on earthly things.*'"[12] Now Reca's brown eyes were rimmed with tears. She caught her breath and continued.

"But at the same time I heard the words, I smelled green

mint. I began hopping like crazy, searching. And then I found it—a luscious, big patch, green and inviting.

"Lamper tried to send a message, but I blocked it out—and just fell on my face and ate and ate." Now tears made a trail down Reca's brown fur cheeks. She covered her face with her paws and dropped her long ears. "Oh, it's so painful to talk about."

Sara stood up and hugged Reca's neck.

"The leaves tasted strangely bitter. And I noticed the mint had stained my paws green, so I knew my mouth was green, too. Wimdos would know."

Sara wiped the tears from Reca's face with her hand and patted her paw.

"I felt so guilty," said Reca. "Wimdos called for me. I bowed my ears to the ground trying to hide, but she kept calling. Finally, I couldn't stand the pain. And I sobbed out, 'I'm sorry. I'm sorry!' It was all I could say. Then Wimdos was suddenly there, stroking my horrid green paws. I cried even more. 'Dear little rabbit, you are forgiven,' she said. 'But it's up to you to take the forgiveness into yourself.'

"For a long time I lay crying on the ground. Wimdos waited. Then somehow I lifted my ears and looked in her glowing black eyes. She smiled and pulled me to her velvet fur and held me close."

"Did you get to go to the Banquet?" asked Sara.

"Not right away. I certainly couldn't go with green mint stains and a sick stomach. In fact, I had to be washed in the river and put to bed. But the next time I was invited, I got to go.

"Child, you are so miserable." Sara dropped her chin to her chest and twisted the corner of her dirty shirt. "I believe you are suffering from Dripe disease."

"What's that?" asked Sara. "Do I need a doctor? Is it serious?"

"Oh, yes," said Reca nodding her head. "It's very serious. This disease is stealing your very life. Have you had any fun lately? Done any dancing or singing?" Sara pulled her shirt tail over her face. "Child, you can be forgiven for not listening to Lamper and eating the cinnamon rolls. But you have to ask for and accept a cleansing."

"It'll hurt me!"

"It will heal you from the Dripe disease, but it's up to you," said Reca.

Sara blinked hard to keep the tears from coming, but she fell against Reca and began to sob.

"Why's everything so hard? It's so easy for Andrew—to give in."

"It's not giving in. It's giving *up*—giving up the disease."

"Oh, I do want to! I hate myself. I'm sorry. I AM sorry. Lamper tried to speak to me, and I wouldn't listen."

"And?" Reca waited.

"And then I—I lost everything—my concentration, Wimdos, my faith, Lamper's voice, and—"

"Your hope and love?" asked Reca.

"Yes. Oh, yes. I lost everything!" said Sara.

Reca began to glow. Placing her paw on Sara's head, she spoke in a strong, deep voice. "By the power of Lamper, you are forgiven. Dripe, leave this child!"

Sara shivered. The light from Reca covered Sara, and a warm breeze blew across her face, ruffling her hair. Her tiny body relaxed as Reca cradled and rocked her to sleep, singing a special lullaby.

> *Cleansing light, warm the child*
> *Who lies here in my lap.*
> *Clean her heart, heal her hurt.*
> *Refresh her in her nap.*

Sara drifted into a deep, but gentle sleep, safely snuggled down in Reca's thick fur. Reca rocked her to and fro.

"Well, what have we here?" asked Teleng. He smiled and turned to his bunnies and Andrew. "Looks as if Sara has given up the Dripe disease. She had a bad case!"

Sara stirred in her furry nest of Reca's lap and opened her eyes wide. Everyone was looking at her.

"How long have I been asleep?" She stretched her arms high, spread her fingers, and yawned. "Oh, I feel so much better."

"Child, look at your hand," said Teleng.

"Why, the scar is—"

Andrew squinted to see. "Pink like mine. Just a pink line."

"Yes, just a reminder now of a time gone by," said Reca. Sara hugged Reca and slid from her comfortable lap.

"Will all of you please forgive me. I've been—well, horribly bratty—especially to you, Andrew."

Andrew ducked his head and grinned. "Aw, let's have our party!" And all the rabbits began to clap and laugh.

BLACK RAIN

WHILE THE LIGHT abandoned the meadow to the rolling smoke, a great party occurred underground in the safe rabbit burrow. After a feast of poppyseed cake and mulberry juice, the children and their rabbit friends danced, sang, and told stories.

Finally, in happy exhaustion, they tumbled into bed to sleep. But even in their safe retreat, the children had restless dreams of being crushed by Snedoms and being drowned by Neam and his Senparps.

A loud knock at the door broke into everyone's sleep.

"I say! Up and about, ol' chaps! The Meadow's full of light."

Squirrel Dink had let himself in and rushed around the room, brushing up cake crumbs with his bushy gray tail. "I'm here to escort the children back to Mrs. Mole's."

Sara rubbed her eyes and crawled out of bed. "Is anything wrong?"

"Wrong? Wrong? Oh, yes, indeed, something is wrong! I came to tell you at the first break of light. Krad's mounting his forces. The whole Meadow's restless. He screams orders to his troops through that horrible, thick smoke, and Snedoms soar endlessly, looking for you children." Sara trembled and shot a look at Andrew. He looked pale and sick.

"But why us?" asked Andrew, trying to make out Dink in the dim burrow.

"Because, pets, you're the ones," answered Dink.

"What do you mean, 'the ones'?"

"Never mind that now. We must be going. Hurry along," said Dink.

"Yes, we'll help you," said Reca. And she, Teleng, and Dink began to glow.

Andrew and Sara stared at the halo of light around their friends. Suddenly, they were full of a knowing—a knowing that the adventure ahead would be the greatest challenge of their lives. And before they faced their future, they needed more training.

The rabbit family hugged and patted the children and followed them out into the Meadow light. "Oh, please, be careful!" said Reca squeezing them deep into her furry chest one last time. A tear splashed on the top of Sara's head.

"Learn your training well. Your help means more to us than you can imagine." Tears brimmed Teleng's brown eyes as he rubbed Andrew's head.

"Come now, pets!" said Dink, and he scurried ahead as the rabbits waved good-bye with their tall brown ears.

The Meadow seemed strange. There were no sounds of woodwinds and strings. There wasn't even a hum or whistle in the air. The children ran trying to catch up with Dink.

"Dink! Slow down, will you!" yelled Sara. But Dink kept his speed.

Andrew stopped and pointed up. "Hey, look at that." Sara shielded her eyes with her hand and squinted through the light. A dark black layer hovered above the light.

"This gives me the creeps," said Sara. "Let's catch up with Dink." As they began to run, the sky split with a streak of lightning. Thunder cracked, and wind stirred up the Meadow.

"We're gonna get killed!" Sara clapped her hands over her ears and stood as if nailed to the ground. Lightning flashed again, and thunder rolled, breaking the eerie silence.

"Come on. Snap out of it!" Andrew grabbed Sara's hand and yanked her along. Sara finally got her footing, and they ran hard.

"Ugh, what's this?" Andrew wiped a wet blob of sticky black from his forehead.

A big splash hit Sara on the head and ran down the side of her face. The drops splashed faster and faster streaming down like thick ink. "Black rain?" asked Sara.

The children ducked under a toadstool and peered out. Trees, grasses, flowers drooped under the weight of the dark, thick rain. As they watched, thunder shook the ground, and the sky seemed to give up to the black thunderstorm coming through the light.

"I—I'm scared." Sara leaned against Andrew. He could feel her shaking. "I'm really scared. And it isn't just the thunder."

"Serious business, this is." Dink stuck his head underneath the toadstool. He was a dismal sight. His fur was soaked and matted with black, dripping globs. "Things are going on up there I've never seen before."

The Meadow appeared to be destroyed—smothered in black. "This is terrible," said Sara. "Everything's ruined—just look at the flowers."

"Terrible, simply terrible," said Dink who loved cleanliness and felt miserable about his dirty fur. Suddenly, from the east end of the Meadow, from Lamper's Mountain came the blast of a trumpet.

"Listen!" Dink cocked his head, and the children came to attention. Out of the blasting sound came a powerful, radiant light beam. It slowly swept the Meadow. Everything began to sizzle and snap. The light rose and fell over the great oaks, sycamores, birch, and pine trees. It beamed around each leaf and blade of grass. Every flower lifted its face to be cleansed. And all the creatures of light who were dripping in black goo stood waiting to be cleansed.

"Look at that!" said Andrew shading his eyes. "Wow! The light's eating up those sticky blobs like candy."

"Out in the open, pets. We need to be light-cleaned."

Before the children could resist, Dink pushed them along with his tail. They felt the power rush as a light beam shimmered over clothes, faces, hair, and fur, beaming them clean.

"Now, that's the ticket," said Dink, pulling at his squeaky-clean whiskers and ruffling his fluffy gray fur. "Whatever happened, Lamper certainly had the last word."

"There's not a bit of that globby black stuff left," said Sara. "The light just cooked it off everything."

"Well, I wonder what's going on," said Andrew, squinting straight into the light. "That dark layer's sure not up there anymore. Dink, can't you tell us ANYTHING?"

"I can tell you a bit," said Dink, as he wrapped his tail around the children. "I think that devil Krad is pulling all his crafty tricks! He's started the WAR, and I'd say he's trying to invade the light. All the more reason we must arrive at Mrs. Mole's as soon as possible. You two, up on my back for a ride."

Andrew climbed on Dink's back and put both arms around his neck. "Hang on to me," he said to Sara as she scrambled up behind him.

The children jerked back as Dink sprang into a run. Andrew gripped deep into Dink's fur, and Sara clung to Andrew's waist. Once settled, they rested as he carried them to Mrs. Mole's. The mystery of Krad's black rain splashing through the light had frightened them both. Each time they met Krad's shocking power, it seemed more awesome.

FINAL TRAINING

DINK STOPPED ABRUPTLY.
"Here we go, pets." The children dropped off his back to the ground. "Follow me now."

Dink squatted down over a small rise in the dirt and, digging fast and hard with his paws, made a hole. The hole opened up to a wider dark cavern below.

"Drop down," said Dink.

Sara half slid and half fell through the hole into the tunnel. Andrew tumbled on top of her. "Watch it!" grumbled Sara. "Where are we?"

"Oh, pardon me," said Dink, and he began to glow so the children could see. "We are in one of the outlying tunnels leading to Mrs. Mole's. She's made many of these burrows underground for safety. And the Named Ones memorize their whereabouts, just in case." Dink's tail stood straight up.

"In case of what? Dink, I need some facts. Can Krad invade the Meadow? And who are WE to Krad?" Sara paced nervously in the hard-packed dirt burrow letting her questions fly.

"Only Mrs. Mole can answer you, chappie. Come this

way." Before she could ask another thing, the glowing Dink scurried down the tunnel, leaving Sara pacing in the dark.

"Come on," said Andrew. "If he leaves us, we won't be able to see." And they both ran after Dink.

After many twists and loops, the tunnel widened to a place where shelves of books lined the walls.

"Come! The main room's ahead." Dink darted into the space beyond the hall, and the children ran panting after him. Mrs. Mole sat at her wheel, spinning in front of a rosy fire.

"We're here, Wimdos," said Sara, running towards her.

Dink stuck out his paw and stopped her. "Shhh." He wrinkled his forehead and twitched his short, pointed ears. They watched Wimdos at work. Her wide clawed foot rocked the treadle of her spinning wheel in a gentle rhythm. "Look at the bobbin," whispered Dink. Out of the air, through her claws, and onto the bobbin spun a yarn that looked like brilliant light.

"Her eyes are closed. Is she in a trance or something?" asked Sara.

"What's she making?" asked Andrew.

"Quiet!" said Dink. Wimdos opened her blazing black eyes.

"Ahh—it's good you are here. Excellent work, Dink. Please refresh yourself with tea." Wimdos's voice sounded like a lullaby.

She left her spinning wheel and, walking to the children, placed her claws on each of them. Looking deep into their eyes with her quiet, serious face, she said, "Are you ready for the last training?" Now her body began glowing, and the children could feel the warmth on their skin.

"I am ready!" Andrew gave Wimdos a sharp salute.

"I need to ask a few things," said Sara. "What's going on out there? I mean, we practically drowned in black goo. And we keep hearing that we're 'THE ONES.' Just what does *that* mean?" Sara's hands trembled.

Wimdos stood in silence, but her claws dug slightly into Sara's shoulders. Sara shut her mouth and looked at Wimdos. Then, sucking in a breath, she closed her eyes and concentrated.

I will answer all your questions in time, said Lamper.

Yes, Lamper, but—but well . . .

Trust me, and trust Wimdos, your trainer. When you see me, all your questions will be answered.

Sara rested her chin on her chest. Wimdos rubbed Sara's head.

O.K., Lamper, thought Sara, *let's begin.*

"Splendid listening, my daughter," said Wimdos. "You have not forgotten."

"What? Forgotten what?" Andrew looked at Wimdos and Sara.

"Listen for Lamper," said Wimdos. Andrew gazed around the room and fidgeted with a string in his pants pocket.

"Shut your eyes and concentrate," said Sara softly.

Andrew closed his eyes. Black wet globs began forming in his imagination. Splattered down on his face, they made thick inky blotches and ran down his cheeks.

"Andrew," Wimdos spoke quietly. Andrew shook away his daydreams and looked at his trainer. "You must control the thoughts and imaginations of your mind. Now try once again. Listen for Lamper's voice."

Barely breathing, Sara and Dink watched on pins and needles as Andrew closed his worrying eyes.

I am your King, said Lamper. Andrew caught the word *King*, and he began seeing a golden crown floating about, covered with bright red rubies and sparkling diamonds.

I am Lamper, your King.

This time the words remained long enough in his mind for Andrew to grab them. *Lamper, you are my King*, he thought back.

"I heard him!" exclaimed Andrew.

"Good," said Wimdos. She sighed. "You need to control your mind even more. Your life may be at stake."

Andrew shivered.

"Come," said Wimdos. "The final training will keep you very busy until you are called out."

"Called out! What does that mean?" Sara pulled on Mrs. Mole's yellow apron.

"No more questions, my daughter. They will be answered, but not by me. But before we go to the training room, there is someone who wants to see you—very much."

A gentle cooing filled the room.

"Ceapé!" cried Sara.

"I've made her a nest—there in the shadow of my own bed," said Wimdos.

Sara rushed to her friend and sank down beside her.

"How are you?" she asked, stroking Ceapé's feathers. She laid her face against the bird's wing.

"Since Dink brought me food from Lamper, I have gained some strength."

"But what about—about your eyes?"

Ceapé sighed. "The same. Where's the boy?" Sara lifted her head. "Andrew, Ceapé wants you. We're over here." Sara whispered to Ceapé, "He can't see well, specially in the dark, since he lost his glasses."

"Ah, yes," cooed Ceapé, and she began to glow.

"Thanks," said Andrew glumly, as he stumbled to Ceapé's nest.

"Don't give up, my friend," cooed Ceapé.

"I just can't seem to overcome my daydreams," said Andrew.

"I know you're discouraged," said the bird. "Training's hard, and each of us has different challenges. Here." Sticking her head underneath her wing, she plucked out two small, sharp-ended feathers. "These are my gift to you. Take them when you're 'called out.' Keep them close, and you'll know my spirit's flying beside you. Remember, give your all, and when your all is spent, my feather will give to you." Ceapé lowered her glow.

Sara wanted to ask Ceapé more about the feathers, but Wimdos was calling them. She gave Ceapé a light kiss, took her gift, and followed her leader.

Andrew looked down at the bird. Looking back at him in the semi-darkness were two milky-white, blind eyes.

Andrew's eyes burned as hot tears blurred his own poor vision.

"Dear boy," said Ceapé, "I can see your face in my mind. Take courage." Andrew tied his feather to the string around his neck that held his precious prism. Then hugging her neck, Andrew spoke a soft "Thank you" into Ceapé's feathers before following the others.

Looking for the light of Wimdos and Dink, Andrew felt alone and afraid. The scent of honey tea flooded him, and his stomach growled.

Oh, brother! Me and my big ideas, he thought. *Sara's right. We need to get ourselves home and out of this mess.* He fingered the cut edges of his prism.

Take special care of your prism, said Lamper.

I will! Andrew shot back his thought. Then he saw Wimdos just ahead.

"Good work, my son!" said Wimdos. "Good work. Now follow me through the wall."

She and Dink disappeared through the wall. Sara followed without a hitch. But when Andrew took a step, he ran smack into solid mass.

"Ouch!" he yelled rubbing his aching nose and forehead. "Now I'm gonna have a stupid bump."

Concentrate, came the familiar word. Andrew doubled up his fist and marched stiff-legged. Wham! He smashed his face against the wall. His nose began to bleed.

"Hey, open up!" He shook the door. "I can't do this!"

Yes, you can. Concentrate, said Lamper.

"Well, you must think I'm crazy! I'm not gonna run

myself into a wall three times!" Slipping down to the floor, he leaned his back against the wall and pinched his throbbing, bloody nose in the dark. The dirt floor felt cold and smelled damp.

Andrew heard something. The hair on the back of his neck stood up. Sliding his feet close to his body, he hugged his legs and squeezed his eyes into slits trying to make out the danger. His palms started sweating, and his skin tingled all over.

Could Senparps get into Mrs. Mole's secret tunnels? He could see them in his mind, surrounding him, ready with their horrible sharp snapping mouths. Slobbering over their find . . .

"Don't do it! Don't! I'm ju—just a little boy." Covering his eyes with one hand, he stuck the other out to fend off the enemies.

"Ohh—" His heart sank as his fingers touched something clammy and damp. "Ohh, drooling Senparps!"

"Sometimes I think you're a frogbrain, kid," said a familiar voice.

"Godo! My gosh! Why didn't you tell me you were out there?" Andrew slumped back in relief.

"Why didn't ya ask me? I told you kids to stay out of trouble, but it looks like you shore didn't listen to me. Whatcha doin' out here in the dark?"

"I—well—they won't open the door."

"Hummm. Cough out the rest, kid." Godo began to glow to get a better look at Andrew's face.

"Well, they told me to walk through the wall. I nearly

broke my face trying. I guess I'm just too dumb. Of course, brilliant Sara went right through."

"So ya figure you'll just sit out here in the dark and rot."

Andrew dug the worn heels of his tennis shoes into the moist dirt. "I think I'd just like to forget the whole thing and go home to something normal," he mumbled. "Not talking moles and frogs."

"Moles and TOADS!" Godo puffed himself up and put out his full glow. "Looka here, kid. There's no such thing as dumb—just different kinds of smart. What's easy for her is hard for you. But what's hard for her is a cinch for you. Now don't be quittin'. Ya just need a little work in concentratin'."

"That's real easy for you to say, but—" A loud snore from Godo cut Andrew's speech short.

"Oh, I guess you're right. I sure can't get any better just waiting for them to open the door."

Closing his eyes, Andrew sat still and quieted his mind. *Breathe out the jitters. Breathe in the quiet.* He looked for the light of Lamper in his mind. *Help me!* he thought.

Rearrange the wall mass and walk, said Lamper.

Andrew imagined the cells of the wall to be liquid and moving. He saw the cells swishing back and forth. Rubbing his bruised nose, he waited just for a second. "Well, here goes."

The first step took him into the solid wall, and in a flash he had walked through—into Wimdos's welcoming forepaws. The mirrors reflected a hundred grinning Andrews being congratulated by Dink and Sara.

"You made it! I'm so proud of you," said Sara. "I knew you could do it!"

Andrew grinned.

"Pull up your shirt," said Wimdos. Andrew dutifully lifted up the ragged bottom edge of his faded polo shirt and looked at himself.

"My skin!"

"Your skin's clean—and glowing. You see, every battle you win over yourself leads to a cleansing victory," said Wimdos. "Good work, my son. Good work!"

Andrew smiled. *It seemed that everyone forgot how bad I failed after I succeeded. Maybe everyone fails during Lamper's training,* he thought. *I sure am getting to know myself!*

WORD POWER

"I SAY, I hate to be pesty about this, but I feel we MUST get on with things," said Dink. "There's so much to teach."

"Right you are. Let's begin with this." Wimdos drew the beautiful light sword from her deep apron pocket and handed it to Dink.

Dink held Ritips high, letting its light beams dance across the training room and bounce against the mirrors. He handed it to Andrew.

"Every move you learn will serve you well. I charge you both to demand excellence of yourselves." Dink's fur bristled. "I will be hard on you, requiring your best. Can't be muddleheaded about this. A mistake could cost—"

"Your lives! And very likely, ours as well," said Wimdos.

Sara looked into Andrew's pale, serious face. She touched his arm. "Together?" she asked.

"Together." His voice cracked.

Dink handed Sara a shield and unsheathed the black sword. "On guard!" The black and the light crossed over their heads. The training resumed.

Between the difficult sword and shield sessions with

Dink, the children listened to deep secrets from Wimdos. They studied the ancient books, practiced concentrating, and grew better at hearing Lamper's voice.

Wimdos and Dink continued to press their students. Every muscle in the children's bodies ached from fencing, and their minds felt numb from thinking.

"Please, Wimdos, I've gotta rest," said Andrew.

Wimdos, glowing like a lamp, pulsed with heat, for she had worked hard along with them. "Not yet. Now think about these sayings. You first, my son. Give me the meaning. *'Wisdom gives strength to the wise more than ten rulers that are in a city.'*[13]

"Ah—well, being wise will give me more strength than ten kings and queens could give me."

"Good," said Wimdos.

"*'The patient in spirit are better than the proud in spirit.'*[14] Daughter, meaning."

"I think I'm learning that one. Being patient is better than acting like you know everything," said Sara

"Yes, and a wise person knows there's always more to know," said Wimdos. "This one, my son. *'It is better to hear the rebuke of the wise than to hear the song of fools.'*[15]

"I think that means that I need to pay attention to what you and Dink tell me when I mess up, not just listen for praise."

"Splendid! Indeed it does. We want you to grow strong and wise. Krad and his dark ones will try to deceive you. You must stay on guard for their tricks!" Wimdos looked at Dink. "I think we'll have tea now. We all need something to eat."

A surprising gust of wind smelling of pine and cedar freshened the children as they lay resting on the mirrored floor.

Dink disappeared through the wall and reappeared carrying a fancy silver tea service on a large silver tray. The children sat up. Cinnamon and orange smells swirled from the steaming teapot. Poppyseed rolls, watercress sandwiches, and bread cut into star shapes were piled high on a clear glass plate.

"Time for a proper high tea now." Dink pulled the lace tea-cosy off the teapot and poured the hot tea into two delicate white cups rimmed in silver. "One lump or two?" he asked, holding a sugar lump by silver tongs.

"Ah—two I guess," said Andrew, as he grabbed for a couple of tiny sandwiches.

"Not so fast, chappie. Wait until you are served." Dink glanced at Wimdos. "I was right. They need feast training, too." He turned to Sara. "Tea, my dear?" Sara wiped her hands on her shirt front.

"I'm dirty from all this work," she said.

"Of course." Dink placed a small silver bowl in her lap. Then from a pitcher, he poured warm water over her fingers and into the bowl. Next he handed her a small linen cloth to wipe her hands dry. "Better?" He smiled. She nodded her head.

On fragile white china dishes decorated with tiny yellow buttercups, he placed the sandwiches, blueberries, and little star-shaped breads spread with strawberry jam.

Putting the teacup up to her lips, Sara made a slurping sound. "Too hot!"

"No, no, that will never do! Let it cool, and then drink—like so." Picking up his teacup, Dink lifted his chin and wiggled his whiskers. Then slowly he sipped his tea. Andrew laughed at Dink.

"You look like some fancy dude in the movies," he said.

Dink scowled. "It won't be at all funny if you receive an invitation to Lamper's Banquet, and you don't know how to eat properly."

Andrew's face turned beet-red.

Before long the children's spirits and bodies gained new strength from the delicious food. And their new energy came just in time.

"Ready yourselves, my son and daughter," said Wimdos. "You have the two most important weapons left. You must learn how to use the power to summon Ritips and—"

"And what?" asked Sara, holding her breath.

"How to use the power of words," said Wimdos.

Before Sara could fire off any questions, Wimdos instructed them to watch. "In a time of danger you may need to call Ritips to you. First you must concentrate." Wimdos closed her black eyes, lifted her nose high, and stretched her broad claws in the air. Glowing like a spotlight, she sang a haunting song that made Andrew and Sara shiver.

> *Come, Ritips,*
> *Sword of Light,*
> *Split the horror*

> *Of the night.*
> *Fly quickly*
> *To my hand*
> *To give me*
> *The Light Command.*

An eerie hush hung over the mirrored chamber as they waited. Then suddenly, the sword, which had been resting in the middle of the floor, began shimmering. As the children watched wide-eyed, Ritips, its light quivering for a moment, lifted off and sailed into Wimdos's claws.

"I say! Good work there, Wimdos," said Dink. "What do you say, chappies?"

"I—well—I can't believe it," said Andrew shaking his head. "It's like the guys I've seen doing magic tricks on TV."

"Yeah," said Sara. "Those guys always have some hidden hocus-pocus to do their stuff. So what's the trick?"

Wimdos stared at the ceiling, muttering. She shook her head. "Lamper, Lamper—I can't believe your children are so . . ." Then shuffling over to Sara and Andrew, she bent close and spoke in a whisper.

"Don't you understand yet? You are being told the ancient secrets of the Named Ones. Secrets full of the true power."

"I guess I sort of get it," said Andrew. "But—"

"But it's not like anything we've known in our life before, so it's hard to believe," said Sara.

"You must accept the way—the way of faith in the secrets of Lamper or else . . ."

"Or . . ." Gulping hard, Sara reached for Andrew and dug her fingers into his wrist. "Or else what?"

"Or else—you'll be powerless. You'll fail in the battle against Krad," said Wimdos.

A chill fell over the training room. It was as if a deeper understanding of what was to come—what they were preparing for—planted itself in their hearts.

"Now," said Wimdos looking at Andrew, "it's your turn." She put the sword in the center of the room.

Andrew rubbed the prism hanging around his neck. He touched the feather beside it. "O.K.—I'll try."

"I will coach you," said Wimdos. "First—"

"See Ritips with my eyes closed," said Andrew. Pushing his mind to control his imagination, Andrew saw the splendid sword with jeweled hilt of rubies and pearls and dazzling light.

"Call her with your mind," said Wimdos. "And sing after me. Come, Ritips, Sword of Light."

Wimdos shuffled back and forth giving instructions. Finally, it came together—imagination, song, and action.

> *Come, Ritips,*
> *Sword of Light,*
> *Split the horror*
> *Of the night.*
> *Fly quickly*
> *To my hand*
> *To give me*
> *The Light Command.*

Ritips flew to Andrew's hand.

Dink clapped his paws. "Good show, pet. Good show!"

Sara stood for her training. Feeling unsure and antsy, she bounced around on her tiptoes. She tried to concentrate. She sang the words after Wimdos, but nothing happened. Over and over again she tried.

"Daughter, you will never be able to call Ritips unless . . ." Wimdos stroked her short whiskers.

"Unless what? This is IMPOSSIBLE!"

"And that's precisely the problem. You need faith that you CAN call the sword. And until you believe, it will never happen," said Wimdos.

"Well, how does it work? I mean, I've never had anything fly into my hand before. I guess I just can't do it." Sara sank to the floor.

"Oh boy," said Andrew. "You walked through the wall and everything. I don't get it."

"Having faith for part of the training doesn't automatically mean faith for ALL the training," said Dink. "Faith is a gift," he said putting his paw on Sara's head, "as well as a discipline. Until your full training ends, we have kept the faith for you."

Dink rolled his eyes at Wimdos. "I believe we must go on. The training period grows short."

"Yes, yes, you're right." Wimdos turned to the children.

"You both must understand the power of words. Krad has the words of death." The children gave each other a knowing look. "Lamper has the words of life. Do you remember the saying, 'Sticks and stones will break my bones, but words will never hurt me'?"

"Oh, yeah, sometimes kids at school yell that," said Sara. She felt more sure of herself. Words were something she knew about.

"Is that true—true that words can never hurt you?" asked Wimdos.

"No!" said Sara. "Nasty, mean words are real killers. Especially if they're aimed at you!"

"Yeah," said Andrew. "Like that time Pete Simons called me a 'stupid jerk' when I struck out playing baseball. I felt awful." Andrew shook his head, remembering.

"You are absolutely right. Words have power—great power to create both evil and good. Evil words bring chaos—within your mind and outside your body. Murderous battles, raging wars, crushing defeat, angry thoughts come from words of greed, fear, and pride," said Wimdos. "Words I won't even put into the air—for these words swirl in the space around us just waiting to enter our minds and to take us over."

"But what about the good words?" asked Sara. "Don't they have power?"

Wimdos smiled. "A good word from a pure heart has great power—far greater than evil words."

"Yeah, like being called 'stupid' made me feel so awful. I thought I'd never play baseball again. But after the game the coach called me over and said, 'Stevens, I like a player who tries. Keep on swinging that bat.' I can tell you, I felt great!" said Andrew.

"Once when I was sick with the measles," said Sara, "somebody called me and said that sometimes kids die from the measles. I can remember being plenty scared. Then my dad sat down on my bed and said, 'Honey, you're going to be strong and well real soon. Just think about picnics and flying kites.' Those words stuck in my mind, and I wasn't afraid anymore."

"I am glad you know about the power of words. Remember the most powerful of the evil words is *hate* and the most powerful of the good words is *love*."

"Yeah, I knew a kid in our class—he was sort of fat. Then somebody saw him picking his nose and, I don't know why, but everybody just started hating him. They called him 'Willy Snot-nose,'" said Sara. "He got to where he never said anything, just walked around real sad and quiet. Then we got this new girl, and she and Willy got to be good friends. She really liked him. Even said she loved him. And Willy changed—started laughing and being real fun."

"Love gave him new life," said Wimdos. "Words of true love are more powerful than words of hate. Always remember word power and think before you let words in or let words out. Speaking—"

A scratching sound on the wall outside the training room interrupted Wimdos's instructions. She closed her eyes. "Enter, Mouse Pohe."

Pohe scrambled through the wall clutching a white scroll close to her. Her tiny gray body trembled, her pink ears flicked, and her long, white drooping whiskers jerked as she tried to speak.

"Out there—out there . . ."

"Catch your breath," said Dink. "You must tell us everything." Pohe swished her long, thin tail and ran around in circles.

"It's terrible!" Her voice squeaked and then fell into a whisper. "Terrible!"

"Pohe, you're safe here. Now tell us the news," said Wimdos.

"It's Krad—it's Krad. His Senparps are snapping. And the Snedoms are hissing." Pohe sucked in a big breath and continued. "And the Undecided Decided are being swayed—swayed to help Krad and keep Tesps on their bodies. Horrible—horrible!"

Pohe panted hard as she finished her story. Dink curled his thick, soft tail around her small body and stroked her tiny, gray head with his paw.

"Sounds to me like Krad's gathering his forces," said Wimdos.

"Did you bring that for us?" asked Dink pointing at Pohe's scroll.

"Oh, goodness—goodness. I'm to deliver this."

She left the safety of Dink's tail and, bowing before Wimdos, handed her the white parchment scroll.

"Thank you," said Wimdos. "This may be it." She turned away from the others and unrolled the scroll. As she read, the fur on her body began to stand straight out and spark with electricity. Then she lowered her head. "I am your servant, Lamper."

She spun around. "The time has arrived. Krad has called

for a duel. And Lamper requests that his children go. Your training is over. The battle is on!"

"Hey, wait a minute." Sara pulled on Wimdos's apron. "Tell her, Dink, we're not ready. I mean, we're just little children!"

"Exactly! That's why you are the ones who must go for the Meadow." Dink talked as fast as he could. "Just remember, concentrate, and speak in the name of Lamper. Never lose your head, or Krad will strike in your weakness. And remember the power of the good and bad words in the air. Block the evil words as they try to come into your mind. Don't listen to Krad's words—*defeat, death, destroy*. When they come around, shout out good words—*joy, life, love.*" Dink fluffed his tail around the children. "Most of all, have faith."

"Faith in what?" asked Sara.

"Faith that Lamper has called you and will help you."

"Come," said Wimdos. "There's one more thing I can arm you with—Lamper's armor. I've been getting it ready." Wimdos walked through the wall holding the scroll. Dink and Pohe vanished with her, leaving Sara and Andrew standing in the dark.

"Well," whispered Sara. "Here we go." She grabbed for Andrew with a damp, shaky hand. "Hold the faith."

"Hold the faith," answered Andrew, his voice cracking. And in the dark the children's bodies began to cast off a dim glow as they walked through the wall.

THE SEND-OFF

THE BURROW ECHOED with the sounds of the children running after Wimdos and the others. When they entered the main room, they found everyone solemn-faced, waiting.

"Come, children." Wimdos motioned Andrew and Sara to the honey-colored oak chest by her spinning wheel. "I've been making your armor since you came to the Meadow— piece by piece."

She unbuckled the silver buckles holding narrow leather straps binding the chest. "I've been storing it here."

Wimdos lifted the heavy lid, and the children blinked hard as they stared into the chest filled with blinding light.

"What . . . ?" asked Sara, trying to make out the contents.

"It hurts my eyes," said Andrew rubbing his watering eyes with his fists.

"Ah—your eyes are open to the light," said Wimdos. "Now that you can see, you may watch me make the last piece of the armor."

Without another word, Wimdos sat down at her spinning wheel and lifted her claws into the air. Instantly, the children could see that the room from floor to ceiling was full of words—words floating in the air. Some vibrated with light, while others hung dark and heavy. As the children studied the air, Sara began reading the words aloud.

Care, steal, disgrace, death, help, fear, kill, cherish, love . . . "I get it!" she said. "Look, Andrew, the good words spark with life and—"

"And the bad words possess evil power," said Dink. "Don't even say them out loud."

Everyone watched spellbound as Wimdos began pulling good words out of the air. Once she filled her lap with words, she rocked the treadle with her broad foot. Then she skillfully guided the words to be spun. The spinning wheel hummed as the glowing thread filled the bobbin.

Once she had enough precious thread, she went to her large wooden loom. Working with her wide claws, she set up for the weaving. Fast as lightning, she worked to weave the thread of light into a magical fabric.

Reaching deep into her apron pocket, she pulled out a pair of long golden scissors and made a few snapping cuts. Then with a silver needle, she sewed in and out in a dashing motion. Her movements were too quick for the eye to follow.

Finally, she held up her masterpiece. Dink gasped. "Shields!"

The shields shimmered in golden light, sending off beams that lit up the room. Pohe covered her face.

"Now, my daughter, my son, come and I will dress you in

your armor." Carrying the two shields, Wimdos seemed to float to the oak chest. "Come, come. Don't be afraid."

The children crept weak-legged toward the mysterious Wimdos and the objects of incredible light. In the brilliance their dirty, torn, faded clothes, Sara's bare feet, and Andrew's tattered tennis shoes looked worse than ever.

"Blessed be these shields!" said Wimdos handing her gifts to each of the children.

Immediately, the children's ragged clothes flamed and burned off their bodies. Before they could scream, they realized they weren't hurt. But both stood naked. They pulled their shields close to hide themselves. Only the prism and feather hanging around Andrew's neck and the feather in Sara's hand remained.

"Here now." Wimdos slipped shirts of light over their heads. "Step in." She held out a pair of pants for Andrew and then another pair for Sara.

"These fit like a glove," said Sara running her hands over the pant legs.

"Of course. They were made for you," said Wimdos. She lifted two pair of shimmering boots from the chest and steadied the children as they pulled them on.

"Now for your helmets. Dink, help me here." On each head they placed a full helmet that fit down on the children's shoulders and came to a high peak on their heads. Narrow slits for seeing and small slits for breathing were the only openings.

"Lift up his face piece," said Wimdos. And Dink shoved up a section of the helmet that pivoted at the jaw and swung up from the chin, exposing Andrew's mouth and eyes. Wimdos did the same for Sara.

"Daughter, you shall carry Lamper's sword." Wimdos placed a wide strap over Sara's shoulder and buckled a golden scabbard to hold Ritips at her right side. "When Andrew needs it, he can call it to come."

"Son, you will be able to see, even in Krad's evil dark, with the light of the armor to assist you. Now, we have readied you the best we can. The rest is up to you."

Wimdos leaned down and pressed her velvet brown fur cheek against each of their cheeks. Dink wrapped his tail around them both, holding their small, trembling bodies next to him. A tear escaped from his brown eyes and fell on Andrew's helmet. He could feel their hearts pounding in their chests.

"Are you so afraid, my pets? Remember," he sniffed, "Lamper goes with you."

"I—I'm glad of that, but it doesn't help my shaky legs," groaned Andrew. "I'm weak all over."

Sara let out a whimper. *I'm too small for this*, she thought.

"Listen to me, and listen to me well," said Wimdos. "Your words have incredible power. The words you say out loud and to yourself. You can be defeated by your own words of fear. They'll come with the force of their heaviness and knock you out. Up to this point you have been in training, but now you are Lamper's soldiers. Choose his words of good power. One last thing. You must take in your commission."

From her pocket Wimdos pulled the scroll Pohe had brought. Holding it in front of her, she ripped it in two—

right down the center. "Kneel little soldiers. Kneel and eat." Wimdos put half of the scroll in each kneeling child's open mouth.

As they chewed, the scroll tasted like honey for a moment before melting like cotton candy on their tongues. But when they tried to swallow, their mouths puckered from an aftertaste of bitter lemons.

"What did we eat?" asked Sara. "I think I feel stronger." She stood up and put her hand on Ritips. Andrew rose and stood beside her.

"I'm ready to fight." His voice was sure and strong. "Death to Krad." Taking a giant step towards the door, he tripped on the toe of his boot and crashed to the floor. He felt his face flush red. "Oh brother!"

Wimdos helped him up. "Don't worry. Real strength from Lamper will come in your weakness. This is Lamper's battle. Now go. Pohe will lead you as far as she's allowed. Godspeed!"

"This way—this way," said tiny Pohe scampering in circles before heading down the burrow.

As they traveled silently down the twisting, narrow tunnel, Andrew's mind raced with a thousand thoughts and feelings. He spoke to break the tension. "Do you think this armor is—well—strong enough to protect us? Shouldn't armor be some kind of metal, like steel."

"Yeah," said Sara, "and bullet proof." She ran her fingers down the front of her armor. "Feels sort of soft and thin like the long underwear I wear ice skating. How do you think

Wimdos made this out of words? It's gotta have special powers!"

"I hope so!" Andrew grabbed Sara's arm and pulled her to a stop. "I don't know about you, but I'm counting on this armor to keep me from getting killed."

"Light—light is always stronger than dark," said Pohe. They stopped as she ran around them in circles. "And that's what you've got." It was then the children realized they were walking in the tunnel by the light of their armor. And Andrew could see—even better than with his glasses.

"Come—come. This way." Pohe hurried around a curve. "Howdy do!"

"Godo," said Andrew as he met Godo's two golden eyes blinking away his recent nap. To greet her old friend, Pohe dashed up and sat on the top of Godo's head.

"I sure did want to see you kids before the fight. I thank ya, Pohe, for bringing 'em by. Wow, oh wow! Would ya look at those classy duds. Pretty sharp!"

"Armor," said Sara. "Wimdos made it."

"Well, like I said—pretty sharp." Godo lowered his wide head and moved in close. "Listen. I've grown kinda fond of you rascals. Take care, ya hear! I'll stand guard every minute keepin' the faith while ya—ya, ah . . ." Godo's eyelids drooped, and he began to snore.

"Come—come. He's finished," said Pohe.

The cousins helped each other climb around the sleeping toad. Just on the other side of Godo was the exit, and they followed their little mouse leader out into the Meadow light.

Sara became aware of the change first. "Oh, my word. What's happened? Look at my clothes!"

Andrew stuck his finger through a hole in his jeans. "Now what?"

Sure enough, now in the light the children were wearing the clothes that *they thought* had burned away.

"The only thing I have left is my feather," said Sara. "If that's all I got to fight with, I quit!"

"Sometimes—sometimes your best defense is not to show your defense," squeaked Pohe.

Sara rubbed her bare foot in the rough grass to make sure her boots were gone. "Is this a trick or something? Everything that seems real is gone. Just when I was believing—"

Pohe wiggled her pink nose. "Well—well, things invisible are more real than the visible."

"How can you say that," demanded Andrew, "when I'm standing here in my wrecked-up tennis shoes with broken laces?"

"It's true. It's the faith of the Named Ones," said Pohe.

"I don't believe you!" said Andrew, and then he felt himself shrinking even smaller.

"Let's just get ahold of ourselves," said Sara. "Not believing is what got me into lots of trouble. And the fact is that NOTHING has been what it has seemed since we got here. Maybe we should contact Lamper." Sara closed her eyes. "Remember. Don't let black nothings fill your mind. You might lose yourself. I know!"

"Yes—yes," said Pohe. "Better try, I always say. Just concentrate and send Lamper a message."

Sitting down in the tall oat grass, Andrew shut his eyes. *Lamper*, he thought. Lamper's light glowed in Andrew's mind.

Trust me. Trust your training with Wimdos. Sometimes your best defense is to hide your defense, said Lamper.

Andrew looked at Sara. Lifting her chin, Sara ran her trembling fingers through her black hair. "Well, do we believe or not?"

"Let's go!" answered Andrew.

The entire Meadow seemed to be waiting for that announcement, for as the children walked on behind Pohe, they not only heard the song of the River Elif, but a sweep of new, powerful music.

"The Meadow's battle song," said Pohe.

In spite of their rags, the children walked with heads held high into the music and through the strong comforting smell of pine and cedar. Along the pathway, Meadow creatures, large and small, clapped and reached out to nuzzle and touch Andrew and Sara. A gray fox, a mother opossum with three babies swinging from her tail, black caterpillars, butterflies, blue jays, deer, raccoons, bobcats, hedgehogs, beavers, a brown bear and her cubs, a white barn owl, and finally, Reca, Teleng, and their eight bouncing bunnies.

The children felt no fear—only purpose, a purpose for themselves and the Meadow creatures, a purpose beyond their understanding.

They journeyed west. Deeper west than they had ever

gone. For a while the animals paraded behind them. The longer they traveled, the sparser the Meadow became. The music faded along with the flowers, and at last there were no more animals with them except for faithful Pohe. Even the music of the River Elif disappeared as the river hid itself by dropping its powerful flow underground. A puff of black smoke rolled across their path, and the putrid smell of rotten eggs filled the air.

Pohe stopped. "This—this is my ending place and your beginning place." Nervously she ran in tight circles around the children. Sara stopped Pohe and pulled her close.

"Thank you for your help," said Sara.

"And your advice," said Andrew.

"We need each other, I always say. Oh—oh, do take care." Pohe buried her brown face in Sara's lap and then darted down the path out of sight. Their last link to Mrs. Mole was gone.

"We're on our own, cousin. Ready or not, we're on our own," said Andrew.

"Oh, no! Look!" said Sara still staring after Pohe.

Andrew turned in time to see the last of the light coming from Lamper's Mountain in the east disappear. Lamper had closed his gates against the evil smoke. And Krad would have the dark.

THE BATTLE

"P HEW! IT STINKS awful!" said Andrew. He pinched his nose shut.

Sara's eyes burned from the fumes, and tears spilled down her cheeks. "It's the smell of evil all right. Hey—what—!"

The ground trembled and rolled wildly knocking the children down flat as it split apart. A hundred yards in front of them they could see an enormous black cave rising slowly out of a deep crack in the ground.

In the middle of the cave, thick black smoke bellowed from the foot of a black stone throne. Surrounded by hissing, drooling Snedoms and their leader, Selfa, the dark Krad sat proudly on the throne. The hood of his long black cloak was draped over his bald head. His eyes glowed an eerie orange as Krad glared through the dark. On Krad's right the Undecided Decided Gered slapped his terrible quilled tail. On his left, Neam stretched his long wrinkled neck, snapping with his vicious mouth.

"I can't see," whispered Andrew. "I wish I had my glasses—or my armor."

"Shhh!" Sara poked Andrew hard in the ribs. Then suddenly the thick smoke surrounded the children and began pulling at them. Andrew tried digging his heels in the dirt. Sara clung to a broken dandelion stem. But the force broke their holds and sucked them to the edge of the cave.

"Help!" screamed Sara. "Somebody help me!"

"Silence! You're in my dominion now." Krad's sharp, curled beak clamped around his words. "Coming to fight me—me, the great Laho of the Meadow." Snedoms hissed and flapped their great awkward wings around the throne. A strong choking smell rose in a cloud from the wind of their wings. The smell mixed with the thick black smoke swirling up from the base of the throne.

Sara and Andrew covered their faces with their shirt tails. Then without thinking Sara said, "Laho's not your name!"

"How dare you speak!" Krad stood, throwing his hood back, exposing his narrow naked head. "I will show you who has the power. WE are taking over the Meadow and setting up the power of the DARK!"

"Never!" whispered Sara.

"Never?" questioned Krad. "You, girl child, tell me—just how do you plan to stop me?" Krad dropped his pointed, bald head back as he howled with a piercing laughter that echoed through the cave.

Then jerking his head up, Krad closed his eyes to narrow slits and glared. His voice rolled out as deep and cold as the middle of an ocean.

> *You are powerless*
> *Pawns of light,*

> *Here to die*
> *By my GREAT MIGHT.*

He slid his bony claw out from under the edge of his cape and pointed at the children who stood clinging to each other from the blast of his evil words.

"Tell me now. Just why would the great Lamper send two ragged children to duel with me? I'll tell you! Because he's eternally foolish. But this time his foolishness will cost him his Meadow Kingdom." Krad threw back his naked head again, screaming with his strange, echoing laugh. Then he cocked his horrible head towards them. His words became sugary-sweet.

"There *is* another way. You dear children don't need to lose your lives. Why, Lamper is putting you in terrible danger. How could he expect two tiny children to face HIS enemy?"

Krad's words turned bitter as he growled, "Lamper is a spiritless coward!" Then he slipped back to his sweet whine.

"Don't be foolish. Join me. We can take over Lamper's Meadow together. Yes, join me. I'll even make you a prince and princess. And you can rule with me. I can give you power—peace—joy. Wonderful wild parties. All the hot fudge sundaes loaded with nuts and whipped cream you can eat. You'll never have to eat squash again." Krad extended his bony claw and began to rock back and forth. His voice rolled in a rhythm.

> *Make it easy on yourselves,*
> *make it easy,*

make it easy on yourselves,
make it easy . . .

Selfa and his gang of Snedoms dropped heavily from the cave's thorn trees and encircled the children. Then they swayed back and forth hissing to the rhythm. The Senparps stretched long necks from their shells and snapped:

Yes! Make it easy on yourselves,
make it easy,
make it easy on yourselves,
make it easy . . .

The chant grew and grew, mounting in power as the pattern of the words swirled around the children.

"No!" Andrew shouted as loud as he could—not so much to make his stand as to shake himself awake from his dream-like trance. "Lamper is the King!"

Sara, with eyes closed and head dropped to her chest, stood rocking back and forth from the hypnotic words. Andrew's shout jerked her awake. She lifted her chin and blinked her eyes open.

"Wha—what's happening?"

"Listen for Lamper," said Andrew

The chanting grew louder and louder. Sara plugged her ears with her fingers, shut her eyes again, and concentrated.

"Oh, no, you don't, you foul child," screamed Krad as he stretched his long, thin neck towards Sara. Sara blocked out

Krad's sounds and centered her thought deep in the silence of her mind.

Lamper, she thought.

Do not listen to Krad's words. These are words of darkness. Lamper's words came clearly to Sara's mind.

Sara nudged Andrew with her bare toe. "His words— don't listen!" Then she faced all the evil eyes and the sing-song chant.

"Stop!" She planted her feet apart and put her hands on her waist. "No matter what you say, we will never believe you. Just the putrid smell tells me this is no place for a party!"

"Yeah, just look at this place," said Andrew, catching Sara's spark. "Dark and terrible. I don't wanta be a prince in this place."

Andrew realized he had stopped squinting. He could see. He looked at Sara. Light radiated from her golden armor, and Ritips hung ready at her side. "Look, Sara!" He looked at himself. From the toe of his gleaming boots to his shield, he stood in full armor.

Krad yanked down his heavy black hood over his orange eyes and let out a shrill wail. "Now you've pushed me too far. I despise light, and my darkness WILL conquer! If you won't be charmed, be cursed! By all the blackness of evil—by the covering of Death himself I say, be cursed! Cursed!"

> *Blind the fools,*
> *Kill their light,*
> *Slash their eyes.*
> *Dark is might.*

From beneath his cape Krad drew a long, black sword with a blood-red hilt. "You miserable warts—hear this and DIE!" Krad swung the sword over his hooded head.

The sword let out a chilling scream, "DARKNESS AND DEATH!"

Wide-eyed, the children gasped. As they jumped back, their bodies slammed hard into an invisible ice-cold wall.

"We're trapped!" said Andrew sliding his hands over the freezing slick wall behind him. Frantically, he looked for a crack, a hole, a space—any way to escape.

"Just one of my little tricks, you disgusting weasels. You can never get away from me!" said Krad swinging the black sword inches from their eyes.

"BLIND AND KILL," it screamed.

"Go through the wall!" Sara's shout reminded Andrew of his training, and in a split second they both went into the icy wall and through to the other side.

"Stay low." Andrew crawled towards Sara and grabbed her gleaming boot. "Krad's—"

Before Andrew could say another word, Krad began howling a stream of evil words. The filthy words mixed with his breath and melted the wall. Then his black, evil form came even closer. Unsheathing Ritips and swinging the light sword with two hands, Sara cut through the evil words and blackness.

"**Let there be light**."[16] Ritips spoke with authority.

"Aiee . . . get that horror away!" Krad's head sank between his shoulders.

"Stab him," said Andrew. "Slash him!" Seizing the moment, Sara dashed at Krad with Ritips and cut his claw.

"Sara, look out!" yelled Andrew. But it was too late. A group of Snedoms rushed Sara from the back, knocking her flat. And just where the sleeve of her armor ended, they clawed and pecked the flesh of her wrist with their savage beaks.

"Save me!" she cried. Then Sara's armor began to glow brighter. The Snedoms pulled back from the light—but not before Sara opened her hand. Ritips spun free, throwing its piercing light through the dark.

"Now death is mine. Ritips is mine! Lamper's Kingdom is mine!" said Krad, clamping his bloody claw around Ritips. "Ah, ahhh!" Krad jerked back, and the air filled with the sickening smell of burning claw and feathers.

"I'll kill for this! Do you hear! KILL!" And he began howling and cursing as he waved his smoldering claw in the air.

"Andrew—call Ritips," yelled Sara.

"Grab them!" Krad crouched low peering from beneath his hood. "I want them NOW!"

Snedoms pressed around the children, hissing, drooling, and flapping their monstrous, filthy wings. Making a large circle, they began to press in closer and closer, spraying out their foul rotten-egg smell.

"Andrew—the sword."

"I'm—I'm trying." But try as he might, the sound, smell, and smothering energy of evil pressed at his mind breaking his concentration. He couldn't call out the words. He reached for the string around his neck and felt for Ceapé's feather.

Krad yelled out his demand.

> *First take the boy*
> *For my own toy!*

The smothering circle opened to let Selfa flop forward, dragging a heavy metal chain. Just as he reached to loop a chain around Andrew's neck, Andrew made a fast jab at Selfa's narrow black eye. Selfa fell back, cursing and covering his head under his wing. Andrew held Ceapé's white feather over his head.

"Back off, just back off!" said Andrew. Sara pulled her feather out and, using the sharp end like a knife, poked at another Snedom. The feather found its mark, and the Snedom screamed away.

"No more of that you—you wretched brats!"

Krad pulled his hood off. His naked neck stretched out like a snake and waved back and forth as he raged.

> *Tesps, come,*
> *Kill the light,*
> *Fight with evil,*
> *Show your might.*

Instantly the smoke filled with buzzing Tesps who had been waiting for their moment under the feathers of the Snedoms and on the Undecided Decideds. The children felt the blind pests hitting their helmets. The Tesps seemed to grow thicker and thicker as they covered the children's heads, piling their tiny bodies together.

"I can't stand it!" screamed Sara trying to hit the Tesps away. "Andrew . . ." Sara's legs buckled, and she fell under the attacking pests. Wrapped in swarming Tesps, Andrew felt trapped like a mummy. He couldn't move.

Sing your song. Lamper spoke clearly. The words came again—in both their minds. *Sing your song.*

"Sara, listen!" said Andrew.

Sara drew in a breath. A song took form inside her—a song she had never sung before but seemed to know. Opening her mouth, she let the first soft note come through.

The Tesps stopped slamming the front of her helmet. Getting to her knees, she sang louder. Then rising to her feet, digging her shining boots into the ground and lifting her arms, she sang the new song with full clear voice.

> *Lamper is the King!*
> *To Him alone we sing.*

Andrew, too, knew the song. The words and music seemed suddenly to have been placed in him. And filled with new strength, he joined in.

> *Lord of perfect light,*
> *The Lord of strength and might.*

The Snedoms and Senparps and the Undecided

Decideds backed away into the shadow of the black stone throne. And the Tesps flew back to hide on the bodies of their hosts.

"Come, Ritips," called Andrew.

> *Sword of Light,*
> *Split the horror*
> *Of the night.*
> *Fly here*
> *To my hand,*
> *Give me*
> *Holy Command!*

And Ritips flew to his outstretched hand. Lifting it high, he readied for a duel. Then Lamper's voice spoke again.

The prism. Fight with the light of your prism.

"My prism!" Andrew felt for his treasure. Pulling the string over his helmet, he held the prism in front of him. "Yeah!" He moved toward Sara. "Keep singing and hold on to Ritips." He put the jeweled hilt in Sara's hands and carefully eyed the light beams streaming from the blade.

"Hold her steady!" He dangled the prism by the string.

Krad, hidden under his hood, broke through the cowering Snedoms and Senparps. He held his black cloak outstretched like a net. "I'll snuff out your light and smother you twin horrors myself!"

Just as Krad moved to toss the cloak, Andrew swung the prism into a stream of pure light from the sword. The light passed through the prism and broke into a rainbow of brilliant yellow, orange, red, violet, and blue. The Snedoms hissed crazily and dropped flat.

"No!" howled Krad. The colors of light fell in dancing waves, cutting across the dark scene. "Retreat! Retreat!" he yelled.

In voices clear and strong, the children continued to sing to their King. Sara held the sword steady, as Andrew kept the prism fixed in the light. They watched amazed as the colors shimmering with life replaced the dark of death.

Krad, slinking from the blast of colors, dragged himself behind his black throne. Neam and his Senparps closed up in their shells. Gered and her Undecided Decideds began gnashing their teeth and shaking in terror.

The Snedoms flocked like flies in retreat behind Selfa. Flopping and panting, they tried to escape by piling on top of their terrified, defeated king. Their bellows and howls diminished to whimpers and then to silence.

The light grew in intensity, melting the mass of evil into an oily, black liquid swirling around Krad. The light was overtaking the dark, when suddenly the cave began to shrink and close. And swallowing up what was left of the dark, the cave sank deep into the ground.

The Invitation

T HE CHILDREN STOOD on the edge of the Meadow, bathed in Lamper's light. Their song became even stronger.

> *Lamper is our King!*
> *To Him alone we sing.*
> *Lord of perfect light,*
> *Lord of strength and might.*

The air filled with the scent of honeysuckle. Green wild grasses and masses of yellow buttercups and black-eyed daisies danced ruffled by a fluttering breeze. Lifting their limbs, birch and eucalyptus and pine trees waved in a gentle rhythm. The sound of woodwinds, brass, and strings lifted from the land to make a joyful noise. And everything that had life and breath began to sing.

As they stood in the music with the light washing over their bodies, the children let the last note of their own song ring in the air.

"Look—our armor's gone again," said Sara.

"I think it'll always be on us," said Andrew smoothing his ragged shirt, "even if we can't see it." Andrew hung his prism back around his neck. It sparkled with color against his chest. "I'm glad I didn't lose this." He felt the cut edges of the glass with his fingertips. "It was the light that saved us!"

"Help me find my feather," said Sara as she began poking around. "I want to take it home with me."

"Yeah, home," sighed Andrew. "Lamper's just gotta help us get home. My folks probably have the whole town looking for us, even dragging Miller's Creek in case we drowned. It's probably on TV news that we're missing."

"I wonder how long we've really been gone? Hey, here's the feather! They're both here!" The feathers, quills sticking in the ground, looked like two white spears. "It's like they're waiting for us," she said clasping their treasures.

They had no need of Sara's map now. They simply traveled east toward Lamper's Mountain. The mountain was ablaze with the light. And although neither of the children said it, both were afraid of meeting such radiance.

They walked on, drinking in the music and thinking about Krad's defeat and about Lamper. The splendid light, stronger than ever, splashed on everything, washing new life over the Meadow as the children passed by. Suddenly, they had a visitor.

"Oh—oh, joy! You've saved us. Wonderful—wonderful!" Tiny Pohe, her long, brown tail flying, scampered in a circle around the children, clapping her tiny paws and chattering. "Follow—follow me!"

"But we're on our way to Lamper's. See, we really need

to be getting home," said Sara. "Seems to me, as dear as you all are, he's the one who can help get us home."

"Yeah," said Andrew, "you can't believe how much my mother worries when I'm late. She's probably crazy by now!"

"Don't—don't worry," said Pohe. "You're at the beginning of the best part of everything. There's no way you can be late when you're at the beginning. But now you must come with me."

"Where?" asked Sara.

"You—you must come to Mrs. Mole's."

Sara shrugged her shoulders. "I guess we should follow Pohe. What do you think?"

Andrew scuffed his toe in the dirt. *What a relief! I don't think I'm ready to climb straight into that mountain of light, at least not without our friends.*

"Well, maybe Mrs. Mole could help us get to Lamper," said Andrew.

"Good—good, you made the right choice," said Pohe. "Now, follow me!" She scrambled down the familiar narrow trail, and as the children followed, the grasses parted at their feet. Looping around an old, smooth-trunked willow tree near the River Elif, the path widened.

The children stopped walking and grinned. Lining the path were the Meadow creatures who had cheered them on their way to meet Krad.

"They—they are waiting for your return. A sign of faithful friends, I always say," said Pohe.

Teleng, Reca, and the bunnies grabbed Sara and Andrew first, and the air filled with cheering, laughing, hugging, and

dancing. Deer reached down to lick them; bobcats and raccoons rolled in the grass; bears and antelope sang together.
Grasshoppers hopped wildly; butterflies and birds darted
about landing on the children. It was a marvelous Meadow
party.

"Cheers, chappies." Squirrel Dink curled his furry tail
around the children. "Climb on my back for a ride home.
Hang on, pets."

As they straddled his back, Dink moved through the joyful creatures on the path, who greeted the children with more
pats and hugs, shouting, "We're free! We're free!"

Overwhelmed with both excitement and fatigue,
Andrew and Sara sank into Dink's thick, gray fur, grateful for
the ride.

"I'm taking you straight away to the front entrance," said
Dink. "Ahh—there's Mrs. Mole awaiting you now." Dink
ran down the mushroom-lined path and stopped.

"Here are the son and daughter of light," said Dink. "Did
an honorable job, these two chappies."

"Thank you, dear Dink," said Mrs. Mole. The children
slid off Dink's soft back and stood dirty and tired in front of
their trainers.

"Good work, my children. You've fulfilled one purpose of
your visit to Lamper's Meadow. You've closed a season of the
Dark and freed the Meadow from Krad's clutches. For now
we are free!"

Pulling the children close to her brown velvet fur, she
gave them a long hug.

"How we all thank you! Now you dears must rest before

Teleng and his family arrive with food. Then we'll sing and celebrate and wait."

"Wait for what?" asked Sara.

"For your invitation," said Mrs. Mole, "your invitation to Lamper's Banquet."

"Oh, I really appreciate everything you're doing for us, but really we can't be staying around for parties. We gotta be getting home," said Sara.

"So could you tell us the way to get to Lamper's now?" asked Andrew. *And just maybe you'll go with us,* he thought.

"You're not ready to go yet," said Mrs. Mole, flashing her black eyes in a knowing way. "Besides, you are far too tired. Now follow me."

Mrs. Mole shuffled rapidly down the burrow like a flashlight in the dark. Coming to a bend in the corridor, she went first, leaving them behind.

"Hey," said Andrew. "I can still see! Wimdos took her light, but I can still see!"

"Look!" said Sara. "You're—you're glowing!"

Andrew stuck out his hand. "Wow!" He moved it up and down, watching the light of his arm spread through the dark. "You too," he said, touching Sara's hand. And then in a moment, under the power of their own light, they entered the main room.

"We made it!" said Andrew.

"Oh, dear ones!" The sweet high voice sent Sara rushing to Ceapé's nest in the shadows. "I have kept the faith with you, and you two freed us all."

"Ceapé! Oh Ceapé!" Sara rushed to her friend and petted the soft feathers around Ceapé's neck. "If it weren't for your gift, we'd probably be dead." Then she turned to Mrs. Mole. "And Ritips, and the training you and Dink gave us."

"And Lamper's wonderful direction," said Andrew. "Seems like it was all of us together." Mrs. Mole twitched her short, stiff whiskers and smiled.

The eight chubby bunnies hopped in the door, stopping the talk by smothering the children with a tumble of hugs.

"They understand that you brought them freedom to play in the Meadow without fear," said Reca, as her long ears danced back and forth. "I've brought you a fine meal of blackberries and bread. It'll hold you over until your invitation arrives."

Reca began setting the table, pouring tiny acorn cups full of honeysuckle nectar. And on the petals of two blue flowers, she placed one blackberry and a slice of warm, sweet bread. Then she washed the children's hands and faces, and they climbed onto their stools at Mrs. Mole's table. It felt good to be cared for, and they ate with great thankfulness.

"Now, to bed with you, little soldiers," said Teleng, wiggling his nose as he looked at the bedraggled children. "You're dead on your feet."

"Oh, no—I'm not tired," said Andrew widening his drooping eyes. "If there's gonna be a party, I wanta stay up. Wimdos, you never did tell us how you got your sight from Lamper."

"Please, please tell us," begged Sara as she slipped down from her seat.

Mrs. Mole laughed, and her pear-shaped body shook

light over the room. "How can I deny you anything? But first you must crawl into these thistledown beds, and then I'll tell you the story."

Sara slid down into the deep comfort of her small bed and fought against her drowsiness. Andrew pulled off his worn tennis shoes and filthy socks and slid his body in bed under a soft blue-flowered comforter.

"O.K., we're ready now," said Andrew, covering a yawn with the back of his hand.

All the bunny babies, Teleng, Reca, and Ceapé snuggled close to hear the famous story. Mrs. Mole cleared her throat and smoothed her yellow apron across her lap as she sat on a small toadstool in the middle of the room.

"I shall begin at the beginning. I was born blind. That is because all moles before me were born without eyes. I lived in a world of darkness, making burrows and tunnels with my wide claws and searching for food from the depths of the ground." She paused and sighed as she remembered.

"I longed for more of life. I yearned for wisdom. But the other moles laughed and said, 'Wisdom? Why do you need wisdom? You were born to be a creature of the dark. Nothing more. That's our destiny. That's your destiny.'

"This made my heart nearly burst with sadness. To think I could only be a creature of the dark." Wimdos stopped to wipe away a large tear with the corner of her apron. She took in a deep breath.

"One day I ventured out of the cold, damp tunnels and into the Meadow. The warmth on my fur felt so good. The Meadow music filled my body. A deep yearning came into

my heart for something—something other than cold darkness." She glanced lovingly at the children. Both of them
were nestled in their beds—already fast asleep.

She went on with her story. "Well, whenever I could slip
away from my family and the other moles of our burrow, I
climbed out into the Meadow. I filled myself up with the
music and warmed myself up in the light. The craving grew
in my heart to leave the darkness forever.

"Then a most unusual thing happened. A voice called
me. '*Come this way*,' it said. The voice was so kind, so loving
I couldn't resist. So I began following the voice. It was a long,
frightening journey, for I was called from the dark but safe
ground into the open Meadow.

"I traveled over rocks, through grasses and flowers, hiding from smoke that choked me, and moving only when I felt
the warmth return. I heard creature noises and music I had
never heard before. But I listened with great care for the one
voice that had called me into the journey. It was that voice I
had to follow—or I would be lost forever.

"I began to travel up—up a steep path. I moved my body
inch by inch on my stomach pulling myself along with my
claws. I thought I could not go on, but always the voice spoke
love and courage into me.

"Finally, after what seemed like forever and with my dirty
fur torn in places, the journey ended. Gentle hands stood me
upright on my back feet. Then over my face came a hot
touch—a burning touch—yes, suddenly . . ." The listeners
stared at their storyteller, as her velvet fur began to glow, and
her eyes blazed.

"I could see! And there HE was—beautiful King Lamper. His voice—his touch—" Wimdos could no longer speak. Giant tears dropped down her cheeks as she remembered.

"And that's when Lamper gave you the Books of Wisdom to read," said Dink. Wimdos nodded her head.

Now all began telling their stories of Lamper, each in turn. Just as Reca was about to finish hers, Godo hopped into the circular room and puffed himself out.

"This is it!" he said waving a long scroll. Edged in gold, it was tied in the middle with a royal-blue satin ribbon. "He asked *me* to bring the invitation to the kids." Godo bugged out his eyes and croaked, waking the children. They sat up and stretched, wonderfully refreshed.

"Git a move on. Lamper's callin' you to his Banquet. Gotta git ready. Climb out of that bed, you lazy guys." The strum of his banjo struck up, and as he held out the invitation, Godo slapped his webbed foot on the floor to the beat.

Andrew took the white scroll, and Sara untied the blue ribbon. Together they unrolled the long piece of cream-colored parchment. The words on the scroll were written in gold.

"What does it say?" asked Andrew studying the invitation. "Here, Sara, you read it."

Sara studied the words intently. "I don't know. I can't seem to make it out." Puzzled, she looked up at Andrew. "Doesn't make sense—unless it's written in lots of—"

"Languages," said Teleng.

"Yes, my children. These are good words to clothe you.

Words of love, joy, peace, strength. Words in all languages,"
said Wimdos. "It's time for more of my spinning." The animals clapped and laughed.

"Can we watch?" asked Reca. "We love to watch you spin
the words."

"Of course you can! Come children. This is what we've
been waiting for!" Everyone circled around Mrs. Mole at the
spinning wheel. All knew what was going to happen except
the baby bunnies. Their eyes had not yet been trained to see.

"Now, Andrew, hold the invitation high and shake it
gently," said Mrs. Mole.

Andrew held the scroll by the top corner and shook.
Golden words lifted off the page and floated about the room.

"Wow! Look at that!" said Andrew.

"Now you, daughter. Take a turn," said Wimdos. Sara
held the delicate paper by her fingertips and flapped it once.
More words sailed into the air. "Make sure you shake them
all off. Each word is precious. We don't want to miss a one!"

Sara shook again. And Wimdos sat down at her spinning
wheel. Lifting one claw, she began pulling the golden words
from the air into her lap. Gently rocking the treadle, she
guided the words and spun them into a yarn of white light.
Everyone watched without moving as she worked her humming wheel. After a long time, every word had been taken
from the air and spun.

"Now for the weaving," she said in a deep voice. She took
the bulging, light-filled bobbin to her weaving loom.
Working as fast as a humming bird's wings, Wimdos began
to weave. Then she drew the golden scissors out of her deep

apron pocket and began to cut. Threading her silver needle with fine light thread, she sewed—lost in her work.

"Ah," she sighed. Then her scissors began flashing again.

"She's finished with one set of clothes," whispered Reca.

Wimdos licked the end of her thread and threaded the eye of her needle. Checking to make sure each piece fit together perfectly, she launched into her sewing again. Her needle and thread seemed to fly. Finally, she slipped the tiny garments over each claw and held them up.

"Oh, how beautiful! How extraordinary!" said Teleng.

"Try them on, pets," said Dink.

"Yeah, them raggy duds you're wearin' ain't gonna make it at the Banquet," said Godo.

Andrew and Sara stared at the gleaming clothes. They were quite different from the armor—soft as down feathers, bright as the moonlight.

"Quickly now. Don't be shy. These are a gift to you from me," said Wimdos. "And from Lamper. Lift your arms high." In a flash Wimdos had stripped off their rags and dressed them in their new clothes.

"Look, my dress fits exactly," said Sara spinning around. "Oh, it's beautiful!" The white dress looked as fragile as a butterfly's wings with its long flowing sleeves. Tied at the waist by a wide golden ribbon, the skirt fell to her ankles. Two dainty velvet white violets dressed her tiny feet.

Andrew ran his hands over the smooth front of his gleaming shirt. "It's so silky!" he said. His soft white pants, belted by a gold cord, barely touched the top of his golden sandals.

The prism hung around his neck on a solid gold chain reflecting yellow, red, green, and purple from the light of his clothes. "What can I say?" he asked hugging Wimdos. "I don't know what to say."

"It's—it's all so wonderful," said Sara lifting her skirt as she danced.

"The Wonderful is still to come," said Wimdos. She bowed slightly from her round waist. "He is still to come!"

THE BANQUET

WHILE THE CHILDREN admired each other and strolled about getting accustomed to the splendor of their new clothes, their friends also dressed up.

"Look at Reca," said Sara. Andrew turned his head.

Reca and Teleng were waltzing around the burrow in clothes that gleamed like a delicate spider web in the sunlight. Reca wore a filmy, long, white silk gown. A spray of white jasmine was tied with white satin ribbon to her right ear. Teleng's three-piece white suit buttoned up with gleaming moonstone buttons. Their soft ears touched gently as Teleng hummed his tune and danced his wife in circles.

Now Mrs. Mole and Dink moved to the music. Mrs. Mole's apron had been replaced by a snow-white gown of purest linen that shimmered as she swayed. A diamond necklace hung around her brown velvet neck. Dink held his furry tail out from under a cloak of shining silver that buttoned at his neck with a large pearl. Tiny Pohe, dressed in white satin, stood beside him. A wreath of miniature wild roses and ribbon encircled her head.

Coming from the shadows, Ceapé hopped towards

Teleng's hum. Over her feathers lay a splendid white velvet cape with silver tassels bobbing around the edge.

"Wow!" said Andrew looking from creature to creature. "Wow, you're all—"

"Transformed," said Sara.

Then Godo let out a cheerful croak. "I do love my fancy garb!" He hopped around the rabbits in his brilliant white waistcoat and trousers. A silver velvet bow tie went around his large toad neck. The baby bunnies took the children's hands, and everyone sang and waltzed.

"Ah, I see we're all ready now," said Mrs. Mole. "We can journey to the Banquet together." Tenderly she patted the bunnies with her claws. "But you dear ones must wait for your invitation. When you are called to be named, I will spin for you—special clothes for each." Teleng and Reca gave their children last minute instructions and big hugs.

"Come on, gang," said Godo, straightening his bow tie. "It's a long hop up the mountain. Better shake a leg!"

"Tell me everything that happens," said Ceapé.

"What do you mean?" asked Sara. "Ceapé, you must come with us."

"Oh, child, the journey to Lamper's would be too hard for me. I can't see the way. Besides, you can bring me some of the Banquet food, and I will be quite satisfied," said Ceapé.

"You're going with us," said Andrew. "Maybe Lamper can help you. Here—" Andrew took the golden cord from his waist. "Put this in your beak, and I'll lead you up the mountain."

"Yes, and I'll follow you. Be brave, Ceapé," said Sara.

"Let's be off!" said Mrs. Mole. And she gathered up her flowing skirt and shuffled down the tunnel, leading the way. Through the tunnel they went—all glowing and white— Wimdos, Dink, Teleng and Reca, Pohe, Godo, Andrew, Ceapé, and Sara.

Climbing out of the ground into the light, they saw hundreds of Meadow creatures along the path dressed in splendid Banquet clothes. As Wimdos walked with her small band, the deer placed wreaths of yellow buttercups upon the heads of the children.

"Look, they're all coming along," said Andrew.

"Oh, yes," called back Wimdos. "Once you're invited to the Banquet, you may come and celebrate forever and ever."

The parade of joyful creatures sang their way up the mountain as the Meadow filled the air with music. The splashing, powerful River Elif lifted its voice as it flowed from the Banquet Hall down the mountain to water the Meadow below. Soon the path ran beside the river.

"Are you doing O.K., Ceapé?" asked Sara.

"Well, all right," said Ceapé softly.

"I can see you're about worn out. Andrew, get everyone to stop." Sara stroked Ceapé's neck. "It's a fact that if you've been in bed a long time, you'll lose your strength."

"Hold on a minute!" shouted Andrew. "We gotta let Ceapé rest."

The long parade stopped. Sara bent near the river's edge, cupped her hands, and dipped them in the water.

"Now sip this."

"You're a kind child," said Ceapé. "And you will be rewarded."

"Ceapé, remember—you saved our lives. Now we're bound to each other," said Sara.

After her rest and drink from the river, Ceapé felt stronger, so the journey continued. The mountain light grew brighter the higher they climbed. Andrew shaded his eyes with his hand. "The light's so blinding I can hardly see." He shivered. "Do—do you think it'll burn us up?"

"It's a strange light," said Sara. "Better not look straight into it."

"Do not be afraid," said Ceapé. "Those who have been called have nothing to fear from the light. But the others—well . . ."

"You mean Krad and his gang? They do hate the light. We've finished him off with it," said Andrew. "That's for sure!"

"They have retreated for now," said Ceapé. "But we must never let down our guard."

The path made a twist and led into a wide clearing close to the mountaintop. A wall of purest gold surrounded Lamper's palace.

"Wow! Look at those gates, will you!" exclaimed Andrew. Through twelve giant shimmering gates, light streamed in piercing shafts down the mountain and over the Meadow below. Through the main gate rushed the river. As it splashed down the mountain, it looked like a wide silver ribbon, winding as far as anyone could see.

Sara and Andrew made the last bit of the climb and stood

breathless before the gates. The Meadow creatures danced around the children and through the majestic main gate. Squirrel Dink dropped back and curled his comforting tail around the children.

"I say! What do you think, pets?"

"Uhhh." Sara had no words.

"Come on. Let's go in," said Dink, pushing them gently with his tail.

Passing through the entrance, they saw the glorious palace. Its golden towers extended into the puffy clouds. Over the main door engraved in gold was the word *Love*.

"Right this way, pets," said Dink as he led them through the door and into an enormous room with walls of cedar. The polished pine floors shone like a mirror. The high ceiling arching over their heads was filled with paintings of birds, flowers, animals, boys, and girls—all living things. Surrounding the room were tall windows starting at the floor and arching at the top with all colors of stained glass. Light streamed through the windows, setting the colors free.

"This is the marvelous Banquet Hall!" said Dink prancing around on his back feet.

The children drank in the sight. Purple and gold banners hung from the walls between the windows. A cherry-red banner on a tall golden staff flew over the white linen-covered table that filled the room. Around the great table each place was set with a crystal goblet and a golden plate.

Delightful smells rose from the steaming platters of food that loaded the table. Apples, bananas, grapes, pineapples, strawberries, and oranges lay piled in silver trays. Huge loaves of fresh bread graced the center of the table in silver baskets. Some of the food looked unusual to the children.

"I don't see any peanut butter and jelly," said Andrew, laughing nervously.

"Oh, the food at Lamper's Banquet table is the finest you'll ever taste," said Wimdos. "It fills your deepest hunger and thirst."

"Mighty fine vittles! Yes, sir," said Godo. The marvelous smells filled the Banquet Hall, and Andrew heard his stomach growl.

"Well, it sure smells great!" said Andrew.

"Are we all gonna sit here?" asked Sara.

"There's room for everyone," said Ceapé. "Everyone!"

"Come, my children. It's not time for the feast yet. We must go to the Throne Room." Wimdos led them by the hand from the Banquet Hall. Dink led Ceapé behind them.

They entered another enormous room. The children could hardly take in the sight. The floor seemed like gold but was crystal clear, and it sang softly underneath them. Holding tight to Wimdos, they walked towards a vast white throne and the light sitting on it.

Sara caught her breath. Andrew trembled. Sparkling water was gushing out from under steps to the white throne.

"This is where River Elif begins," said Wimdos. She led them closer towards the figure on the throne.

Sara's mind tried to form a question. *Are we looking at a star?* But as she drew closer, suddenly all the questions she had ever had seemed answered. For now she could see the intense beauty of the light, and she knew that every time she had seen a bit of light, she had been with Him. The familiar scent of cedar and pine swept over them, and both children fell on their faces.

"Lamper—Lamper," was all they could whisper.

"Arise, my daughter. Arise, my son," came the voice from the terrible light. This was the voice that had led them on their journey. The voice was so full of love, so kind that even though they shook like leaves in a storm, they lifted their eyes and peeked out at Lamper.

Now a rainbow of colors danced in wide bands over His head.

"You're like—like my prism," said Andrew.

"Come, my little ones." Lamper's voice sounded as powerful as a thousand peals of thunder and, at the same time, as gentle as a lamb.

Climbing to their feet, the children stood before the King.

"Do you have a request of Me before we go to the Banquet?"

"We do," said Sara. She turned to Ceapé. "Our dear friend has been blinded—blinded because she saved us. Could You—Sir—well, could You heal her?"

"Do you believe I can?" asked Lamper.

Sara was silent. Then she spoke. "I have no doubt that You can make her see again."

"Untie her cape and bring her to Me."

Sara took the golden cord from Dink and unsnapped the white velvet cape, letting it fall to the floor. Then leading

Ceapé, Sara approached the throne with fear, but Ceapé
began to sing.

"My brave, brave little bird." The King reached down
and lifted Ceapé somewhere into His light. They could still
hear her singing, but they couldn't see her in the powerful
light.

When He let her go, she flew in circles and loops, cooing as she went. Finally, she landed, first rubbing her feathered head on top of Sara's head and then placing her wing
around Andrew.

"Look into my eyes, children. I can see!" Ceapé's milky
blind eyes were now golden and bright with seeing.
Astonished, the children blinked at each other.

"I want you both on either side of Me." King Lamper
stood up and walked down the steps, throwing his pure white
light and rainbow colors everywhere. Sara and Andrew
timidly moved to each side of the shimmering light and
walked beside Him into the Banquet Hall. As He neared the
table, all the Meadow creatures from the smallest to the
largest danced and sang for their King. He sat at the head of
the table under the fluttering red banner. Andrew sat on His
left, Sara on His right.

Lamper filled His golden plate from the platters of marvelous food. Then He served each of the children from His
plate. He poured a sweet-smelling red nectar into the crystal goblets. Lifting His goblet high, His voice booming, He
made a toast.

"Enjoy. Love. This is the Banquet of Light."

The Meadow creatures sat down, and there was a place for everyone.

What fun they all had! Their laughter was like music, and their food, except for some of the fruit, was different from anything Sara or Andrew had ever tasted in their young lives. Sweet and delicious, it satisfied them completely. Andrew smacked his lips.

"This is wonderful, King Lamper. I could eat this every day."

The King laughed, and everyone at the table was sprinkled with His light and color.

Sara sipped the red nectar from her goblet and let the flavor sit on her tongue. "What a great party!"

King Lamper laughed again, and everyone laughed with Him.

A pair of snow geese began to sing a round. Groups of animals joined in until all the guests were singing.

> *Love is our King.*
> *May all our hearts sing.*
> *Love is our King.*
> *Lamper is our light,*
> *May all our hearts unite.*
> *Lamper is our King!*

Some of the creatures got up and began to twirl and skip for joy as they sang. At the end of the round everyone cheered and applauded.

Then the King stood and moved among His creatures,

spreading His marvelous joy as He touched them one by one. Laughter rippled about Him as He enjoyed His creatures. They laughed in return from the sheer joy of His presence.

Full from the feast and Lamper's love, the festival guests began moving into small groups, trading stories about Lamper, Krad's defeat, and the children who fought him. Some ambled off to enjoy the King's flower gardens. Others joined in playful games on the velvet green lawns under the spreading fruit trees near River Elif.

They felt no need to hurry to their Meadow homes. The thick, dark smoke had been forced to retreat, and King Lamper had no need to shut His gates against it any more.

All this time, Andrew had been squinting to see through the light at the King's form.

"Maybe He's an angel, or a living sun," said Andrew. "Can you figure out what He looks like?"

"He's so bright that I can't make Him out. And besides I have a feeling I shouldn't even be allowed to—to look at Him." Sara ducked her green eyes.

"Are you having a glorious time?" asked Wimdos, stopping to catch her breath as she came dancing by. "This is the grandest of all the Banquets, because Krad has gone down. I AM very proud I was allowed to train you."

"Oh, Wimdos!" Andrew hugged her around the waist. "I will miss you—if we go home."

"You will find that we will always be a part of each other now," said Wimdos, as she gently rubbed the top of Andrew's head with her powerful claws. "The wisdom I have given you will always remain with you." She caressed Sara's cheek. "Remember—always—"

"I've been so anxious to go home," said Sara, "ever since I got here. And now, somehow, I feel like—well, like I am home. And dear Wimdos, you've taught me so much. I've been such a jerk sometimes. I don't know how you and the others could forgive me. How can I ever thank you?"

"We've all been forgiven much," said Wimdos. "My daughter, look on others with merciful eyes and be gentle with their hearts. And you, my son, serve others in truth and light. And tell them the story of King Lamper. These are your gifts to others on their journey. Look alive now. King Lamper is calling for you." Wimdos hugged them close and then turned them towards their King.

THE NAMING

KING LAMPER, BATHED in brilliant light, swept ahead of the children toward the Throne Room. They followed.

"I sure am glad Wimdos dressed us up in these white clothes," whispered Sara smoothing her skirt.

"Yeah, I have the feeling His light would burn off anything else," said Andrew. "Will you look at that! He's walking on the river without sinking."

The King laughed, shaking His light and sending the colors bouncing around as He walked on the River Elif and up the gleaming white stone steps to His throne.

"Now, My son, My daughter." King Lamper's voice resounded through the Throne Room. "You received My call and accepted My training. I am pleased with you!"

Andrew bowed his blond head. "Sir, forgive me for saying this," he said in a whisper, "but I really botched things up, and I'm terribly sorry." He looked up into the terrible, wonderful light, and his words came spilling out. "I mean, Wimdos and Dink taught us to concentrate and use Your sword, and the others don't know, but I nearly fell apart."

"And," said Sara joining in the confession, "if it weren't for Ceapé's feather, we would have completely failed. I almost lost faith in everything I'd been taught." Sara's eyes rimmed red with tears.

"I know," said Lamper with a voice like a soft summer breeze.

"Were You with us all the time—in the light of the sword and our armor?" asked Andrew, already knowing the answer.

"I was, My son. And I forgive you both for all your failures. My reward is for your hearts—hearts willing to serve Me, your unseen King, even if you stumble over your boots."

Andrew grinned.

"I have invited you to eat from my Banquet table, and you have come. Now receive a secret gift which will make you part of a whole—your new names.

"Sara Katherine Stevens." King Lamper's light rose and shimmered as He stood. Sara stepped out of her velvet slippers. And walking barefoot on the cool glass floor to the foot of the throne, she knelt by the rushing water.

"I now name you **Ditlegh**. Rise up. Delight in the life I have given you."

Ditlegh felt something warm and smooth in the palm of her right hand. She stood and, opening her fingers, she found a round, white stone with her new name, **Ditlegh**, burned into it.

"Andrew Jonathan Jeffrey Stevens." The King's voice rolled like thunder, and the ground shook under Andrew's feet. He unbuckled his golden sandals, stepped towards King Lamper, and lay flat on the crystal floor.

"I now name you **Nojey**. Rise up. Enjoy the life I have given you."

Nojey rocked back on his knees and opened his hand. A smooth, white stone lay in his palm. Written across it in gold letters was his new name, **Nojey**.

"I know your desire to go home," said Lamper, His light quivering over the room.

"Oh, maybe I was wrong," said Ditlegh. "I mean, I really love it here, but I feel so torn."

"There are people who would miss you. People you must go to—and love." Lamper's voice whispered like a misty morning.

"I want to stay!" said Nojey. "I belong here now. I want to stay with You, King Lamper, and Wimdos, Dink, and—"

"I know, Nojey. I know. But my desire is for you to go. I have much more for you to do. This one thing you must know—I will never leave you. Never! Come!" The great Light reached out to Ditlegh and Nojey and pulled both of them deep into Him. It was then they saw Him, really saw Him. His love was even stronger than His light. And He wasn't like the creatures of the Meadow. Why, He had a body like human beings! Yes, they could see their King, and they were like Him.

"Now you know why you were the ones to face Krad," said King Lamper. "You are made in My image."

There seemed nothing else to say. They simply pressed deeper and deeper into Lamper's love. Deeper and deeper and deeper. Complete and satisfied.

The Return

The basement was dark except for the beam of white light focused on the prism, breaking into a brilliant rainbow. The other prism lay on the cement floor where it had been flung.

"Oh," Andrew groaned. And finding himself flat on his back, he rolled over and slowly sat up. "Sara?" He grabbed his cousin's leg and yanked it hard. "Sara!"

"What happened?" Sitting up, she leaned against a dusty chest. Sara ran her fingers through her dark hair and then shook her head to clear her mind. "Boy, I had a crazy dream about a mole and rabbits that talked and—"

"And Lamper?" asked Andrew.

Sara jerked her head up and studied her cousin in the dim light. "How'd you know that?" She slid closer to him.

"Because—well, I had the same—dream." Andrew stood up and flicked on the basement light. He spied two white dove feathers at his feet. Then he opened his hand, exposing a white stone with the name **Nojey** engraved in gold letters.

Sara spread out her fingers. **Ditlegh** was written on her stone. "Did it really happen?" She stood up to check out her size. "I've stretched out again. That *is* a relief. Are my clothes O.K.? Hey, I even have my tennis shoes." Sara jumped up and down around Andrew, talking and laughing.

"Do you believe—believe we went to Lamper's Meadow?" asked Andrew.

"Of course I believe. Look at these stones. They're proof

if I ever saw proof. Look, you even have your ol' baseball cap back." Andrew pulled on the bill of his cap.

"Well, what do you know?"

"We'd better find your glasses and get home," said Sara. "No telling how late it is."

Andrew looked up at the buzzing electric clock on Mr. Maxwell's basement wall. "It's 4:02 P.M. I bet we've been back at least two minutes. Must not have spent any time away." Andrew laughed. "Can you believe that!"

"Say!" Sara looked directly at Andrew. "How can you see the clock without your glasses? You aren't even squinting."

Andrew took a slow look around. The sledge hammer with its split handle, a brown oak chest with brass pulls, the broken brass lamp in the far corner, the roll of baling wire hanging on a rusty spike—he could see every detail.

"I can see! I don't even need my glasses. Whoopee!" he shouted. "Lamper! Thank you!"

And into his mind came a laughing voice—a voice he knew well.

You are welcome, Nojey, son of light. You are very welcome!

NOTES

1. Colossians 1:17 (NASB)
2. John 12:36a (NASB)
3. John 12:46 (NASB)
4. Proverbs 15:1 (NASB)
5. Proverbs 3:3a (NASB)
6. Proverbs 12:15b (NRSV)
7. Proverbs 17:22 (NASB)
8. Proverbs 27:8, 10a (NASB)
9. Isaiah 60:1a (NASB)
10. Ephesians 5:8b (NASB)
11. Matthew 6:22b (NASB)
12. Colossians 3:2 (NIV)
13. Ecclesiastes 7:19 (NRSV)
14. Ecclesiastes 7:8b (NRSV)
15. Ecclesiastes 7:5 (NRSV)
16. Genesis 1:3 (NASB)

(NASB) New American Standard Bible
(NRSV) New Revised Standard Version
(NIV) New International Version